ALSO BY RAYMOND KENNEDY

My Father's Orchard

Good Night, Jupiter

Columbine

THE FLOWER OF THE REPUBLIC

Raymond Kennedy

The Flower of the Republic

ALFRED A. KNOPF NEW YORK 1983

THIS IS A BORZOI BOOK
PUBLISHED BY ALFRED A. KNOPF, INC.

Library of Congress Cataloging in Publication Data
Kennedy, Raymond A.
The flower of the republic.
I. Title.
PS3561.E427F59   1982   813'.54   82-47834
ISBN 0-394-52539-6

Manufactured in the United States of America
First Edition

To Gloria

THE FLOWER OF THE REPUBLIC

PART ONE

Delectable Mountain

The professor was in the next room.

"Other people listen," he was saying. "He doesn't. This February was the first Groundhog Day in thirty-eight years that I didn't spend with my wife, and now *he,*" he cried, "comes dragging home, four months after the fact, pulling a long face, and regretting, I suppose, he doesn't have a warrant for his father's arrest."

A shout of laughter went up.

"Have you ever seen the roses of September blooming by the thousands all along the grapevines in the old paddock? Have you?" the professor cried. "Because I have. I saw it thirty-eight years ago. Ten thousand roses came out overnight to see your mother. The paddock was a shower of roses. A hundred people gasped when she came out the side door of the house. Her skin was like translucent ivory. She was a vision in white! What will the bridal pictures tell you? That I looked like Bronson Alcott? That the poplar leaves were falling in September? That Reverend Winslow touched Mommy in a way that was not seemly for a man of the cloth?"

Abruptly, a young cadet in spiffy gray military costume marched past the open door, fitting his leather-billed cap to his head. The professor shouted after him.

"You can't court-martial me for being deserted," he cried. "I mean to say, you can't shoot me! You," he said, "have everything! You have youth, vigor, brains! You have a future. You have solid prospects. You'll be commissioned! Beautiful women will want you. You'll have money and a nice home. You'll have children who will love you. After all, it isn't only the blue-collars who experience domestic upheaval, you know. It happens."

Professor Prudhomme shot into view in the taproom doorway, a picture of manic ebullience—shirttails out, cigar jutting, gray brush-cut hair gleaming like a thistle. He swept his cigar downward in a gesture meant to draw attention to his rumpled trousers and lumpy shoes.

"Is this," he cried, "the gentleman of parts you remember so well? Life has changed! What's the matter with you? We'll find her. You've got to have a little faith. A little leaven leaveneth the lump, remember! It's summertime! I'll bet right this minute your mommy is somewhere up in the high latitudes, up Canada way, spreading the good word from wickiup to wickiup! She had a hankering for blue skies! For wide-open spaces!" In a sudden access of joy, the professor flung his cigar at the wall. "Can't you just see her," he cried, "smoking the chieftain's pipe and reading 'em excerpts from Increase Mather? From *Wonders of the Invisible World?*" he shrieked. Laughing hoarsely and coughing, Professor Prudhomme turned and lurched into the taproom. As he did so, his eye was arrested at once by the sight of a woman of truly spectacular proportions, the biggest woman he had ever seen. She was wearing a straw sombrero and sat atop a bar stool by the window, clutching a pilsner of beer in one hand and scowling at herself in the mirror back of the bar.

"Up in Ryegate, they know who I am," she was saying. "They know me in Randolph and Readsboro, and they know me up in Eden Mills." She planted her glass on the bar top. "What about you?" she threw out drunkenly at the barman. "Do you know who I am? Because I'm going to tell you one time. I'm the gal who comes back. You lie to me," she said, "then I come back." She discovered Professor Prudhomme watching her in the mirror. "I don't care if you're as old as the hills," she said. "You could be decrepit, actually decrepit," she touched a finger to a titanic breast, "it doesn't matter to me. I come back!" Turning on her stool, she looked the professor over from head to toe with contempt. "Well, look at we here," the big woman said. "Look what the cat dragged in."

Professor Prudhomme smiled, his gold tooth twinkling as he stifled a laugh. "You will forgive my intrusion," he said, and started toward her, "but I could not help noticing, Madam, the astounding resemblance you bear to someone who is very precious to me."

This declaration caused the woman to put her head back and loose a roar of laughter. She swept the sombrero from her head. Her face, uncovered, showed itself to be round and ruddy and possessed of dark slanted eyes. She was beaming at him. A pink flush rose to her cheeks as she reached a hand underneath her breast and dealt the professor a look of unforgettable lewdness. "And who would that be, if it isn't Mommy?" She turned away in ecstasy. "Where on earth," she thundered, "do they find them?"

"My mother," the professor objected in cordial tones as he advanced toward her, "is no subject for barroom humor. You are talking about one of the true venerables of New England, a chairwoman of the old Atheneum, an early shareholder in Radio Corporation of America."

"Give Mr. Einstein a drink," said the woman to the bartender with a shout that revealed a spirit of good fellowship toward a man capable of speaking up to her.

"I was speaking of my wife," the professor continued, "a woman whom I revere not less, but more, than my own sacred mother." At close range, Professor Prudhomme found himself the target of an enormous, insidious smile. Ebony lights glittered in the pupils of the woman's eyes. She was laughing soundlessly at him.

"I never met a bum who wasn't looking for Mommy," she said as she reached and transferred a glass of whiskey from the barman's hand to the professor's.

"In point of fact," he explained amiably, while stealing a prolonged peek at the Amazonian bosom by raising his glass and affecting to examine its amber contents, "I am on the road today in quest of my wife. I crossed the border from Massachusetts not an hour ago. Does that sound to you," he smiled, "like the itinerary of a feckless fellow?" He stole a downward glance at the woman's billowing loins. "We are not a bum," he said. "We are a professor."

The big woman crossed her legs effortlessly, and allowed the toe of her sandaled foot to press insolently against the professor's leg. "I never met a bum who wasn't a walking apology for the human race, and every bum," she said, "is either a professor or a poet."

"I am a poet, too," he admitted.

"A bum is like your common Norway rat," she explained, while pouring beer from a bottle into her pilsner. "I'm an exterminator, and I know what I'm talking about." She signaled the barman for another bottle. "Because of me, there isn't a rat in Montpelier. I could run for governor. I know rats, and I know bums."

Here the professor intruded upon the great woman's discourse to salute her with his glass.

"For one thing, a bum doesn't vomit," she said. "A bum doesn't, and a rat doesn't. Did you ever see a rat vomit? You will never see it. A rat does not vomit." She nudged him rudely with the sole of her sandal. "When was the last time you vomited?"

"I've never vomited in my life. I get sick," he conceded, "but I don't vomit."

Professor Prudhomme's reply sent the big woman into peals of laughter; her bosom and arms quivered awesomely. "I swear," she boomed, "you're one of the purest, most delicious bums I've ever seen in my life! That tooth!" she cried. "That mouse on your eye! Those pants! Mister, I can spot a bum like that." She snapped her fingers in his face. "It could be the way he buttons his fly, or how he keeps close to a wall when he walks, or maybe the welts on his forehead where he hit the sidewalk. Or maybe he looks at me like he wants me to take down his pants and paddle him. There are a hundred ways, and a different one for every bum." She finished her beer and belched noiselessly. "Listen, a man came up to me in the old railroad station up in St. Johnsbury one night about five years ago, a man dressed in a nice-looking suit, new shoes, Bulova wrist-watch, an Order of the Masons on his finger—a respectable businessman type, don't you know, with a briefcase and a rolled-up umbrella and a spanking-new white raincoat, and before that man could open his mouth, I said, 'Mister, you are a bum! You are a cheap, low-down, son-of-a-bitch grifter who hasn't slept indoors since they invented radio, and what's more,' I said to him, 'if I had a benny or two in my purse, you'd strip naked for it right on this bench!'" With a shout of laughter, the woman reared back and threw out her arms in a massive gesture to betoken a human being awe-smitten by her powers of perception. "The bum was fucking paralyzed! Flabber-gasted that I saw right through him. He couldn't've guessed how I'd done it if he had a lifetime to think about it." The big woman waved her hand in deprecation.

Professor Prudhomme, enjoying his beverage, offered a companionable observation. "I mightn't have thought you could have accomplished it, either," he said and drank.

"A hundred things about him," the big woman explained in an intimate tone. "To begin with, he was whistling 'The Donkey Serenade,' which is an all-time favorite pop tune with bums. He took a Herbert Tareyton cigarette out of a Chester-field pack. He cupped his match when he lit up. There was no crease in his hair from his hat. His shirt collar was bothering him. He watched the trainmaster from the corner of his eye. His shoes squeaked. His watch was stopped. He smiled too much. He stole peeks at Mother's tits." She drummed on her breasts with her fingertips. "Every bum, don't forget, misses Mommy. He was all wrong," she said, "he just didn't fit. And when you don't fit," she explained portentously, "you are a bum. I could write a book about bums." She reached and poured from her pilsner into Professor Prudhomme's empty whiskey glass. "There's your four types of bums." She enumerated them on her fingers. "There's the boozehound bum, the mama's boy, the bookworm, and the pillhead. That's all of them. There aren't any others. The others are lunatics," she said, "schizos, wristcutters, glassheads, firebugs; or else, they're freaks—runts, big heads, pink eyes, syphs, you name it. I like bums," she explained. "What I don't like," she said, "is the disease."

"Disease?" The professor, chewing on an ice cube, glanced up. He studied the big woman's eyes—beautiful eyes, long-lashed and Oriental. She had turned her attention to the barkeep, and put down a five-dollar bill.

"You have rats here," she said, and pointed to the mop board beneath the window. "I can see their grease tracks all the way from here." She turned to the professor. "Rats run in a groove," she said. "You lace their runways with cyanide."

When she got down from her stool, she showed herself a head taller than the professor, while the frame of her body exceeded his in every dimension. She favored him with an impressive smile. Dark lights swam into her eyes, her moon face glowing a rich peony pink. "I ever see you out west of here, out around Olympus or Cuttingsville," she said, "I'll beat your head into a blue mass."

. . .

Professor Prudhomme watched from the taproom window as the great woman lumbered in the rain up the footpath to her tourist cabin on the knoll, a little house with a blue door and blue shutters. He stole out after her and made his way stealthily up the hill to her window. Indoors, a shape moved about ponderously among the shadows, that of a naked back and buttocks, as the woman paced to and fro, slowly, about the cabin, with the measured movements of a mastodon. The rain rattled on the professor's field jacket, while at his feet a steady jet of water erupting from a rainpipe engulfed his shoes. At last, he took himself round to her door, and rapped. After an interval, the blue door swung inward.

The afternoon light in the doorway, combined with the soft glare of a set of pink-shaded lamps, revealed a cozily furnished interior. The big woman was nowhere to be seen, however, although her presence behind the open door could have been deduced by a small child. The sombrero lay atop the crocheted bedcover. There was a Boston bag with brass fittings, a white ironstone pitcher, a drinking cup of the same issue, and, most curious to his eyes, a long-stemmed clay pipe protruding from a glass ashtray on a nightstand.

He listened to the rain hissing on the roof of the cabin, and after a moment more he stepped up, as soundlessly as he could, crossed the threshold, and peeped behind the door.

Indeed, the big woman was standing there, a bedsheet drawn hastily over one shoulder in the effort to conceal her exuberant bosom and loins within its folds.

Her voice came in a whisper. "I knew you were a bum."

Professor Prudhomme smiled with renewed self-assurance. The spectacle of one colossal breast billowing forth from the sheet, right before his eyes, gave him to realize the true volume of her person.

"I knew you'd follow me," she added, hoarsely.

"Madam," the professor began, "there is not a man alive more capable or desirous of treating you with honor and respect. I climbed the hill just now merely to offer an apology for the disreputable condition in which I find myself today. Not only are we not a bum," the professor continued with a garish smile as he moistened his lips, "but we once enjoyed some considerable vogue abroad for our literary attainments. This costume," he signified his field jacket and baggy trousers, "is not so much our academic raiment as the uniform we like to put on when we are playing the wandering bard. Nor is it entirely empty of historical meaning. These herringbone trousers—given me most kindly, I should add, by a relation to Miss Emily Dickinson—once formed a major article of attire in the skeet-shooting kit of Mr. Rudyard Kipling of Brattleboro." The professor leaned backward and extended his left leg a trifle to display the cut and weave of his pants. His violet-ringed eyes gleamed moistly above the grin frozen on his face.

"If you try anything," she muttered.

"I am, Madam, delighted, also, to discover such a charming disparity between your public and private selves—the one so frank and challenging to adventure, the other so demure, really, and so feminine."

"To me," she said, emerging warily from behind the door, clutching the bedsheet in a pink fist, and mincing past him, "a bum is just another stripe of vermin."

"Next to you," said Homer Prudhomme, "a bum is a creature that lives in the ground."

"You've probably heard of me," she said. "I'm Pansy Truax."

"I have heard of Pansy Truax," he replied, grinning.

Miss Truax picked up an ironstone mug containing whiskey and downed a manly draught. As she came by the professor, a nipple the size of a blossomed rose peeped out at him from its setting inside a snowy fold of the sheet. The amplitude of her breasts was breathtaking. Reaching behind him, Professor Prudhomme sent the blue door swinging shut.

"No bum ever dared touch me," the woman said. "In Pusan, you could pick up little gook gigolos at a nickel a throw, but I didn't. Gooks!" she shouted. "Little pinboys specially trained to give you a good time for the price of a candy bar. Why, they'd lick you into a lather just for openers!" Her voice resounded inside the ironstone mug.

"I didn't even know you were in the war," he said.

"I kept myself pure for some lummox up in Vershire for three solid years. I come home," she said, "and find him sacked out in bed with his cousin." Pansy showed the professor a balled fist. "They remember me up in Vershire," she said.

"You were in Korea?" the professsor said.

"Wherever there are bums," Pansy said, "they all know me. If it wasn't for pride in my outfit, I wouldn't have had a crock to show for it."

"That was certainly some kind of army." The professor smiled.

Miss Truax winked. "That ain't no bullshitting," she said. "We policed up the brass every morning at the front. That's the kind of army we were. You won't see an army like that one again."

Pansy drank deeply from her cup while Professor Prudhomme admired the round, pink contours of her upraised arm.

"I was as pure," she said, "as the driven snow. That scum didn't have the decency to write and tell me. Some deer season," she winked ominously, "he'll forget and stray his way into the hills up around Barnard or Olympus, and I'll feed him a thirty caliber—right here." She set the tip of a stocky index finger against the bridge of her nose. "I'll disembowel the son of a bitch!" she shouted. "I'll drag his carcass behind my Eighty-eight Olds from here to Montreal!"

"I knew a man from Vershire," said the professor, wishing to deflect the big woman from dwelling too much on her harsh moral recipes. "He had a three-legged horse and a pepper gun. Jack Hoarty was the name. Jack was a minister of the Anglican faith, and he went round the countryside on that three-legged horse of his, calling the neighbors to the fold while discharging his pepper gun in the direction of demons that only Jack himself had an eye to see. It was Jack Hoarty who claimed to have bound my wife to her own father in holy matrimony, back in twenty-nine."

Miss Truax stood wide-legged before him, a fist on her hip in the attitude of a harbor-straddling colossus.

"Your wife married her father?" she said with disgust.

"That was the scuttlebutt." He shrugged.

"What's your name?" She watched him narrowly.

"Homer Prudhomme," he replied.

"Okay, Prudy," she said, "you go over there and get me my pipe and my Hankey Bannister, and turn out the lights."

"Your pipe?" he said.

"And my whiskey," she commanded him melodiously. "And the lights."

Professor Prudhomme fetched Miss Truax her long-stemmed white clay pipe, which the big woman packed with one hand while gazing at him with basilisk eyes.

"I like you, Prudy. I like someone with a mouth on him," she said.

Her breasts rose and fell before his eyes with a soft, oceanic swelling.

"Take your clothes off," Pansy Truax said. "I want to see what I'm getting."

. . .

Sunday, the eighth of June, was a day of great airiness and luminosity. Twice during the afternoon the patrons of the Northern Lights Bar and Grill hastened outdoors, drawn forth on each occasion by sudden violent commotions on the hill, by shoutings and thunderings and the reports of glass breaking. The little tourist cabin rocked on its foundation. Each time, as abruptly as it had begun, the riotous interlude abated. The summer sunlight reasserted itself. Butterflies appeared above the hedges by the road. In the forest behind the row of cabins, a partridge drummed exuberantly, his wing-tattoo forming the perfect plaudit upon a matchless New England sky.

Monday came and went without so much as a stirring forth of either tenant from Miss Truax's humble cabin. The blue door remained shut and locked, the curtains drawn. Tourists walking past the door heard their two laughters billowing from within—his a raucous, ear-splitting shriek, hers a mellow baritone as she chimed in, their two laughters climbing in counterpoint to a delirious crescendo.

"That poor benighted son of a bitch!" the professor was heard to shout. "Why, he wouldn't have strayed twenty feet from those pigpens if Venus herself had beckoned to him from a cloud of love-barm!"

The sound of the happy, entwining laughters echoed under the pine trees along the highway.

"I'd've gone him one better!" Pansy Truax boomed back. "I'd've nailed his nuts to my bedpost!" She gave then a jolly shout. A crunching of broken glass could be heard from underfoot as she marched about inside. "Anyone ran out on me," she said, "I'd chain him under my outhouse!"

"Well," the professor's voice dropped into a chastened but judicious tone, "you cleave to an Old World code of justice, don't you? Not that I could ever condone government by the knout."

"There's a quality about me," the big woman boasted, "that

you'll learn to appreciate. You'll like the way I operate. You'll
like knowing," she said, "that Pansy Truax isn't spendthrift
with her property. You'll feel more loved. My father used to
lock my mother's hair in the buffet drawer whenever he went
out. People like being kept under lock and key. It keeps them
out of harm's way. Prudy," the big woman's voice changed
inflection, "I'm glad it was you. I needed a little encouragement." Pansy's voice was gruff with embarrassment, as, once
again, she could be heard treading about heavily on the cabin
floor.

"Frankly," the professor was heard to reply at this point,
"your maidenhead caught me quite by surprise. Who would
have guessed you were a virgin?" A mirthless laugh escaped
him. "Of course," he continued, "I realize how pitifully insig-
nificant a part I could ever hope to play in a life as prodigious
as your own. I am, after all, no Prometheus. It is enough for
me," he suggested humbly, "to have been Johnny-on-the-spot,
so to speak, at your coming of age. Let it be noted down in
the annals of Green Mountain legendry," his voice climbed in
irony, "that it was I, a simple wayfarer, trudging about the
hills in search of his absconded wife, who was selected out of
the blue to participate in this unearthly transaction. Why do
you suppose," he added rhetorically, "oysters are required to
ingest a little sand in the making of a pearl? Or gold made
somehow more goldlike through the introduction of a bit of
dross? I ask myself these questions," he said, "when I contem-
plate the working out, Madam, of your own sweet passage
into womanhood."

An hour after dawn on Tuesday, Pansy Truax emerged
from her cabin, her face flushed with happiness, her arm
draped languorously over Homer Prudhomme's shoulders. She
came forth to encounter the morning. Professor Prudhomme,

wrapped up in her embrace, darted suspicious glances to left and right as Pansy marched him down the hill and put him in at the passenger's side of her Rocket 88 Oldsmobile. After cramming herself in behind the wheel, and before turning over the engine, she reached and pulled him up to herself. The professor struggled at first against her brazen advance, but gradually yielded to her amorous urgings, and even allowed her, while kissing him, to probe with her stout finger inside the sensitive ring of his rectum, and, onward from there, onto the soft ridge anterior to his testicles. The woman's finger fondled and kneaded his flesh with authority.

He thought to wonder at the spectacle he made of himself, and even considered the effect such a display might have upon his post at the college. But after a moment or two longer of Pansy's rhythmic kneading, he gave himself over with a soft moan, and relaxed against her bosom.

Miss Truax could not have chosen a fresher, more vibrant morning to chauffeur the professor up the long mountain road to her home in the forest. Mile upon mile, the gravel road wound its way higher and higher amid a wild luxury of evergreen and flowering shrubs; the air all about was scented with the fragrance of the tall hemlocks that closed off the sun. On either side of the road great boulders, covered with moss, appeared as in a petrified avalanche. At hairpin turnings of the road, deep sunlit vistas opened out with revelatory suddenness, chasms of pure space.

The big woman was wearing Professor Prudhomme's army field jacket as a souvenir or trophy of their three days and three nights of lovemaking and brawling, while he, her chief prize, nestled under her arm, his bare chest and shoulders covered with lipstick smears and plum-colored bruises. His lover, he was now forced to admit, was a bully, a hot-tempered, domineering egoist who hit first and asked questions later. Like many violent types, she had a mawkishly sentimental side to her, too, as in the way she regarded her virginity as the purchase price of his eternal soul.

After nearly an hour of climbing, the Oldsmobile nosed its way out of the forest onto a vast mountain meadow lying golden and treeless before them, and overlaid from one end to the other with a delicate mantle of wild flowers. A mile off, against the distant wall of the forest, stood Pansy Truax's stone house, solitary and forlorn, its outbuildings fallen in ruins, a special atmosphere of desolation borne in upon the place by the sheer height of the sky, by the whiteness of the sun, by the black palisade of pines that stood back of the meadow on all sides like an encircling army.

Professor Prudhomme gazed out upon Miss Truax's skyey ranch with an awakening in his breast of a nameless foreboding. He stirred and sat up.

Pansy squeezed his shoulder and smiled upon him in the crook of her arm. "Hope you're not getting tired of Mother's tits already," she said.

At twilight, Pansy Truax and her lover had their first meal together in the stone house, a luncheon of bread and ham and olives served on pewter plates with tin cups of warm milk on the side.

"I didn't bring you up here," she reassured him, "because I needed a cook or a housekeeper, or because I'm horny seven days of the week. I want to make you happy, Prudy. I'm going to take good care of you. I'll keep you dressed up nice, I'll give you pin money for notions, and once in a while I'll take you to the pictures. You understand I don't want you to do heavy work up here. If there's any lifting to do," she said, "I'll do it. You'll sweep the place out, chop some firewood, tote some water, and milk the cow. You can keep a little garden, too. Just remember that Mother is down in the valley working for the two of us."

Professor Prudhomme smiled insanely. "I haven't lived on a frontier in about two hundred years," he said.

"If you start thinking about liquor or about tramping around the country looking for a handout, just remember that you belong to Pansy Truax now and that no harm'll come to you. Another thing is, don't go into the woods by yourself. There are a pack of dogs in there, mean brutes, too, and they'll go for anything that moves. I know 'em. Some come from this place. Blue is in there, and Sweetheart is in there, and Tray and Bullet, and three or four others. If you see any strangers," she cautioned Homer Prudhomme in a quiet, reasonable tone, "just come into the house and lock the door."

"Do you know what I'm reminded of?" the professor put in.

"I'll be gone eight, ten hours a day," she said, "so you'll have all the time in the world to prettify this place. You can bring in flowers if you want. You can put up a curtain or two. There's a treadle sewing machine out back, in case you're mechanical-minded. Mostly," she added, and moistened her lips suggestively with her tongue, "I'll want you to be fresh as a daisy for me when I come home at night."

"Do you know what I was thinking?"

"A time will come soon," she continued, throatily, "when you'll be out in the fields in the hot sun, and you'll be listening and listening, just waiting to hear the purr of Mother's car coming up the mountain. You'll be thinking about me hour after hour, about my toes and my nipples, about what I'm going to be doing to you in bed after dark."

"I can understand why they call it Delectable Mountain."

"I don't want you up half the night reading mail-order catalogs, or mending, or sewing, when you're supposed to be in bed," she said. "I might as well tell you, too, I like you to be considerate, Prudy. You don't come to bed at night talking about your aches and pains and your headaches and such when you should be getting undressed and looking cute as a button for me. So fetch me my applejack now," she said. "I want to talk to you."

"Do you know what I'm reminded of?"

"I'm going to tell you a thing or two about this mountain. Someday you'll love it up here the way I do. This is virgin wilderness, Prudy. You won't ever want to leave. You won't have to worry, either, about my running out on you like she did, your missus. I'm not built like that. I kept myself clean for twenty-nine years, so I know what it means. I won't scoot off on you, and I won't be down in the valley chasing after prong every night, neither."

Miss Truax got to her feet. "I'll build us a fire," she said, "while you clear away the table and straighten up in here. Then you can join me in the parlor. You don't have any pots or pans to do tonight. I didn't want you to spend your first evening scrubbing. When you're finished in here, put out the lantern. I don't waste kerosene."

When Professor Prudhomme appeared in the parlor door, Pansy was comfortably established in her great birch divan by the fire, her pipe and applejack in hand, a blaze flaming in the chimney. She was puffing at her tobacco with end-of-day contentment.

Homer Prudhomme's gaze floated upward from the sight of Pansy's cyclopean breasts shimmering in the firelight under the black cotton of her great nightdress, up to the crude, smoke-blackened ceiling joists.

"Le Corbusier," he said, "would look long and steady upon this place, believe me."

The firelight touched Miss Truax's hands and her sandaled feet, and made a ruddy moon of her face.

"I'll start at the beginning," she said, puffing at her white, long-stemmed pipe. "I may be rough and ready, but I've got feelings, too, and I stick to my word. I won't deny that I get excited sometimes when you're close by. Well, you've got them shapely legs on you," she said, "like I expect you've been told before."

"I haven't," he said, without equivocation.

Pansy took up a stone jug of applejack and replenished her tankard. The blaze in the chimney grew tall, revealing the rough fieldstone walls of the room. "Far as I'm concerned, you're my mate, and I'm going to look after you. It's not going to be all work and bedtime, neither. You've got a beautiful mind there in that head of yours, and I don't want it to go to waste. Types like you," the big woman said, "can get a taste of some hot loving, and next thing you know all they're doing is fucking around the clock till there's nothing left of their brains. There's a fellow down the mountain here named Mr. Nigel French, a so-called gentleman with a college degree," Pansy spat out the words, "who's turned himself into a regular little whore. Mrs. French owns about six corporations, she's head of the county Republicans, got a picture-book farm, a stable of Arabians, and about fifty cunning foxhounds, and *he*," she said, "is down in a parking lot in Pompanoosuc getting himself gang-fucked by a bunch of good-time college girls from Middlebury! The poor woman marries him, puts him through college, buys him fancy clothes and a whole library of books, and now she's got a first-class slut on her hands who's batting his peepers at anything that moves in a skirt. Whenever I drive past the French place, if he sees me, he comes hotfooting out to the road and sticks out his thumb!" Pansy gave a shout of laughter. "I wouldn't let him near my cow!

"I know something about lice, Prudy, and about every kind of termite and roach and skin crab there ever was. But nothing under the sun can carry disease like a fucked-out bookworm!"

Pansy Truax's body shook with mirth. Leaning, she knocked out her pipe.

"Get me my tobacco," she said. "It's on the kitchen shelf by the fishing tackle."

She struck the bowl of her pipe several times against her palm, then blew into the stem. Professor Prudhomme appeared lost in reverie.

"You're a frisky pecker," Pansy said, "till someone tells you to do something."

"But not in anger!" Professor Prudhomme raised a staying hand. "Not in loathing," he said. "Not in revenge, or anything so comprehensible. Just the simple mindless fury of Hell's own princess, the fury of sin, the fury of her own.foul daddy. She buried her teeth in his abdomen, tearing at the flesh just as the old cockroach was acquitting himself!—Jesus, in mid-air, I should suppose!—the sperm going up like soap bubbles! She loved and ravished him to exhaustion, till he lay on the sodden floor at her knees like a soaking newborn calf waiting to be licked dry by its dam.

"That night," said Professor Prudhomme, "the mother of the house, her mother, came down with tularemia, then diphtheria, and was gone in a week, during which time this maiden of the labyrinth moved to the foot of the table, took charge of old Marjorie, the cook, finished her mother's crocheting, moved down from her attic room, and took to wearing the mother's cocoa and ivory wedding gown to Sunday dinner. She sat opposite the old fornicator, he in his carven chair, and she in hers, with the candles going between them, and she looking as freshly bathed and cosmeticized as the ladies of *Harper's*! Her black reptilian eyes shining upon him! She was in Hell now. Her soul was as black as the old gaffer's. She gave up school. She read Jonathan Edwards at breakfast. She grew three inches in five months. She was thirteen years old."

On Friday night, Pansy took the professor down the mountain to a fishermen's bar.

"He can't dance on the tables," she announced, "but he can talk."

Homer Prudhomme took over instantly.

"In my boyhood, we witnessed the end of a bucolic age as old as civilization itself, a sweet rural way of life. But I couldn't tell you what it was like anymore than I could recreate for you in language the scent of hay, the smell of horses' flanks, or the squeal of a sleigh on packed snow."

"Give him something that you serve to the ladies," said Pansy to the barman, to an eruption of laughter.

"Every day was a lifetime," Professor Prudhomme said.

"Give him a sloe-gin fizz," said someone.

"Give him a Shirley Temple!" Pansy roared.

"I wish I could spend a thousand afternoons," said the professor, "exploring just one northern meadow."

Pansy tossed down two silver dollars. "And a Hankey Bannister highball for me."

"Or find myself haying with my father and the Ballou boys, with the horses standing in the shade of the butternuts, and Ida, my mother, coming up from the house with a galvanized bucket and dipper, or earlier than that," he said, "when I was just a little shaver myself, with my sister Lucy running at

Mother's side, her long white frock picking up points of hay at the hem. That world," he extended his arms, "is as dead as the Roman Empire. Our farm was the last farm on the last road. It was in the nature of farming that every farm was the most distant, most isolated, most solitary of all. Dispersal was the name of the game! And that made the men different, you see. It made them natively more ornery—just as I," he said, "am more ornery than I need to be."

"Getting his rocks off really sets him going," Pansy shouted in gigantic tones to another happy outburst.

"His mind was bigger, and his soul was bigger." Professor Prudhomme gulped down his drink and sent his glass skimming up the surface of the bar. "It was in the nature of the fabric, the atomic structure, the nuclei farther apart. Today, I'm obsolete. I could have been born in the city of Ur ten thousand years ago. My soul is out of date. Next to your typical chain-driven, nose-picking Amherst-American pinhead, my soul is a sixteen-cylinder Pierce Arrow! I'm too wide for your roads!"

Pansy cupped a stout pink hand underneath his buttocks. "He's got some life in him," she said.

"I'm extinct!" he added.

"He fucks like a rat on fire!" she said.

"I was talking," said the professor, "about the human spirit. Physically, I'm robust. Sound as a roach, if you must know. I can still run like the devil. I can put a hundred and fifty pounds over my head. Do you know who taught me how to backstroke? Not fifty miles from here? Johnny Weissmuller! John had a summer place down in Monson, in Massachusetts. Mrs. Prudhomme had relatives down there. Fact is, Peleg Emerson taught school there years back, until the day he took it into his head to steal Priscilla from her father."

"She married her father, didn't she?" Pansy winked at the others.

"That was years later," said Homer Prudhomme.

"He's talking about his wife," Pansy said.

"Peleg was Priscilla's cousin," the professor went on.

Pansy Truax raised her glass. "To fishing."

"Peleg was a little runt, trim but phlegmatic, about the size of Bertrand Russell, but rattier in the face. Priscilla was about fourteen at the time, add or subtract a few months, but even then a strangely affecting young thing. Gangly and a bit toothy still, and bony in the arms and legs, you know, but awesome in an indescribable way. Of course, by then, she wasn't just *living* in Hell, she was practically presiding there. Sitting at the foot of the table like a little Gibson girl but with a few Aubrey Beardsley touches of the brush, she and old Dana on a first-name basis, if you know what I mean, but Daddy was still Daddy. Horses," the professor said, "suffered heart attacks when he appeared in the stable door. The king of Hell doesn't wear gold trinkets or winged sandals, believe me. He wears denim overalls encrusted with excrement. Dana had a little go-cart to which he harnessed a team of hogs, a couple of spanking six-hundred-pound Chester Whites, a gift for Priscilla, and of a Sunday afternoon they would take to the air, father and daughter, wheeling along in the sunlight. Pluto's own jaunting car!

"Imagine Peleg descending into the bowels of Hell to rob old Blackleg, not of his daughter," said Homer Prudhomme, "but of his bride! Nevertheless, one August afternoon, into this purple subterranean kingdom, there appeared a young gentleman of education and refinement. He wore a high starched collar with a wide cravat of pearl and black stripes, a fashionable stickpin, a London hat, a Boston costume custom-tailored, and ankle boots buttery soft. Peering in at the farmhouse window of the front door, Peleg proceeded to announce himself with several sharp taps upon the oval glass with his stick of malacca and bone. At once," Professor Prudhomme straightened up at the bar and affected a portentous tone, "the skies overhead turned a deep wound color. Lightning forked! A drumroll of thunder unfolded over the darkened land.

"The interior of the house," he said, "was darker still, as she, the girl, Priscilla, Apollyon's own princess and queen, admitted her cousin into the parlor. The old swineherd was at his prayers, just his shoes and filthy white ankle socks showing through the doorway."

The professor laughed softly to himself and accepted a Rosedale cigar from the fisherman beside him at the bar. He puffed luxuriously, his eye focused on the glowing tip. Satisfied, he took down the cigar and looked at it.

"Peleg Emerson—a man of university training, author of monographs on the subjects of Monson granite, Guilford slate, and Proctor marble, and first-cousin to the black-eyed bride and daughter of Hell's own regent—had come to call. In the course of the evening visit, old Dana sat in his big fire-chair. Sat with closed eyes, the eyes moving darkly behind the listening lids, while cousin and cousin, girl and young man, sat, one to his left," the professor gestured gently, "one to his right— and during the progress of which time the heavens over Amherst poured down lightning and rain, and Peleg's discourse took, gradually, a nefarious turn."

Professor Prudhomme brought down his chin in punctuation.

Pansy stood now behind him, her arm about his waist, her hand flush to his belly, her big-brimmed straw hat above and back of his own head forming a great circular shadow that eclipsed his features.

"The cheek!" cried the professor. "The gumption! The vaulting ambition! The divine irony, of course, lay in the sheer futility of it all. For the black-eyed maiden, you see, was but recently initiated into the complex enticements of paternal love. She," cried Professor Prudhomme, "was perturbed at Daddy Pluto's sleeping in his chair as their customary bedding time rolled around and past. She scarcely heard her cousin's whispered deceit. She didn't hear it well enough to construe its sinful intent, that's for sure, for she told me so. She first noticed, instead, the sight of Peleg's gaping mouth. She sat at her father's feet, trilling her fingernails up and down the father's naked shank beneath his trouser leg, playing a little harp song of love there upon his person, when her eye flew from Peleg's stricken face up, up, *up*," cried the professor, "to the source of terror itself—namely, to the gripping, wide-open eyes of her fearsome father, who sat, wide awake, glaring down with black menace upon the surprised Peleg! He was caught in the scorpion's claws! Peleg's left hand, which he was on the point of introducing into his inside breast pocket, for the purpose of showing Priscilla the two train tickets he had purchased to effect their escape to some faraway city, froze in its place.

"The poor wretch sat transfixed, like a block of stone, as the father arose, and, with trailing suspenders, betook himself darkly from the room. The girl, still curled up on the floor with her legs folded beneath her, watched her cousin in fascination during the short interval of her father's absence, her attention riveted to his pointy, petrified face. The man couldn't move! He was terrified! She kept her eyes glued to Peleg's eyes, behind which glassy stillness she fancied she was able to divine a sort of high-speed cinematographic process going on. Peleg's life," said the professor, "was flashing before him. Fascinated, Priscilla even moved a trifle so as to put herself directly in the way of his vision, and was sitting thus, studying her suitor closely, when old Dana came back indoors, soaking wet from the storm, carrying a long-handled shovel."

Pansy gave a knowing, throaty grunt.

"Peleg's eyes moved once," said Professor Prudhomme. "They flicked upward in a horror of beseechingness into the eyes of the oncoming father. The girl did not glance up, but wished to record the look in Peleg Emerson's eyes at the precise instant of philosophical recognition, at the very instant of doom, since the father was indomitable anyhow, and she saw only, from the corner of her eye, the sudden glitter and flash of the shovel coming through the lamplight and smashing down into Peleg's patent-leather head."

"Jesus Christ," said Pansy.

The professor showed his listeners a be-patient hand.

"Peleg," he said, "got to his feet. His head was streaming blood, but his face was not changed. It was white as a dish. Only his eyes had altered. He was no longer thinking or remembering anything. He was quite dead to all that. The poor devil passed between the two of them like a zombie and marched outdoors, where he fell full-length on the paving stones by the summer-kitchen door, the rainwater carrying the blood away.

"There was lightning, there was thunder. There was a tumult that raged and blew all night long—and in the morning Peleg was found sitting outdoors on a milking stool, completely disheveled. His clothes were ruined. Everything about him was ruined. His hair was parted both ways—this way," Professor Prudhomme indicated a vertical line running from the back to the front of his skull, "and, also, more severely, this way." He drew a line crosswise from ear to ear.

"Peleg," Homer Prudhomme said, "was sitting now on the legendary chair of forgetfulness, the chair of Pirithous. Why, he couldn't differentiate east from west! The man didn't know South Amherst from Moonbeam, Ontario!"

"He was lucky to be alive," someone said.

"There was nothing lucky about Peleg," Professor Prudhomme corrected. "His season in Hell was just getting under way. He had just arrived, so to speak.

"Old Pluto's justice was a killing justice. He gave out the story that Peleg had been hit by lightning. It was taken as a function of Christian grace that the old scorpion made a place in his own home for Peleg, considering that Peleg was once a wicked suitor. For his atrocity, Peleg was moved into a tin cottage next to the pens, where he slopped hogs for no pay for twenty-four years, until he was killed in the great hurricane of 1938, when his meager house blew down upon him. That was one story. Whereas others said it was the news of Robert's birth in the summer of the same year, the receipt of that letter from Mrs. Prudhomme and me in Vienna confirming Priscilla's motherhood, which sent the father steaming up the hill at the height of the hurricane, intent upon some target for his wrath. Either way, it was a godsend for Peleg. It got him out of the world. I *knew* Peleg!" The professor clenched his fists in the air. "I saw him work. I listened to him more than once singing his strange ditties. The poor bugger could even socialize a little, hanging about the hired hands whenever there was work to be done on the hill. But never once in all those twenty-four woebegone years did the fellow stray one step from those pigsties. Sometimes, mornings, you would look up at the hill, with the low-lying clouds trailing their vapors through the endless maze of ramshackle huts, the backs of hundreds of pigs gleaming, and there, in the midst of the tangle of wire and hogs and huts, you saw the silhouette of a solitary man going dismally among them. That was Peleg. Whenever Dana Emerson came by—or even his daughter, for that matter—Peleg would run slobbering into the shadows and cower there till the human presence was gone. He was just an idiot, you see."

"And nobody helped?" inquired some party.

"In those days, it was not so uncommon to herd people into pens. He kept reasonably warm. He had a roof over his head. There are some things," said the professor, "I can't explain to you. It was she, the girl, who found the two yellow railway dockets in his pocket and nailed them to his door. Was she remorseful? Who can say?"

"You asked her, didn't you?" Pansy bellowed.

"Do you know," the professor replied in a philosophical

vein, "I never did. But right this minute, in some forgotten corner of the universe, you can bet that old Daddy Dana's got Peleg by the scruff of the neck and is holding him underwater."

At closing time, a brawl broke out in the fisherman's bar, and to no one's surprise, the giant woman with the straw sombrero was right in the middle of it. Someone in the room had made a crack about her companion. The bartender was running back and forth behind the bar with a peewee baseball bat in his hand, threatening to use it on the combatants, but was apparently loath to give up the mahogany in front of him and come out in the open. Pansy had her dukes up, and was shuffling toward her opponent in that peculiar sidewise style of the professional prizefighter. The patrons of the bar stood back in a silent ring, watching somberly as one of their fellows circled warily about her.

"Come to Mother," Pansy cooed, her two fists revolving very slowly. "Come on, pussycat," the big woman crooned in a voice that portended ruin. Without taking down her eyes, Pansy tossed her hat to the side, and continued to stalk her man, her fists rotating slowly when, suddenly, darting forward with a dark countenance, she let fly with a perfect barrage of blows that caught her opponent as unprepared as had he been sleeping. The big woman was upon him like a lion, with a sharp combination of punches that buffeted his head every which way and sent him rolling along the bar, toppling stools as he went down. Someone else leaped into the fray, going for Pansy from behind with a beer bottle, an assault that led to a general melee, the big woman taking on all comers. Within minutes, she was cleaning house.

In the early morning hours, while driving home up the mountain, Pansy fell into a nasty recriminatory mood, turning ugly glances upon her lover.

"You buy him a gin fizz," she said, "and in no time flat,

he's the talk of the town. I got myself the belle of the ball! What were you doing in there? Wiggling your backside at somebody cute? We all know what you're good at."

"You're likkered up," said the professor.

"Can't cook," she grumbled drunkenly. "Can't clean. Can't even make a bed!" She leered at him in the dim interior of the automobile. "You want to be down in Brattleboro or Keene, shimmying and shaking, I suppose. Dining and dancing! I know what you want. You want me to pull over and knock you around some so's I can feel sorry for you!" Pansy cupped a lighted match to her cigarette without taking her eyes from the road. "You want me to mark you up!"

PART TWO

Tup, His Pilgrimage

Everyone present was familiar with the story of the "talking professor" who had vanished mysteriously in early June while motoring north in search of his runaway wife, so his return to civilization created quite a stir. Mrs. French, it seemed, was galloping her favorite Arabian up a steep logging road in the forest one August afternoon when she spotted what appeared to be a gray-haired Caucasian male darting furtively through the underbrush not thirty feet in front of her. Spurring up her mount, Mrs. French let out a sporting whoop and overtook this tattered individual with a dashing display of horsewomanship that sent her half-naked quarry sprawling headforemost on the forest floor. By nightfall, Professor Prudhomme found himself the center of attention in a distinguished circle of well-to-do art lovers and intellectuals, the summer cognoscenti drawn from the neighborhood and now gathered in Mrs. French's drawing room. He was wearing a handsomely tailored linen suit, Italian silk shirt, and crocodile shoes from Mr. Nigel French's own wardrobe.

Mrs. French, a woman of very advanced years, but possessed of the face and figure of a college girl, sat, looking both fragile and exquisite, in a massive yellow embroidered chair. Her black eyes gleamed with an oily shine as she contemplated her treasure trove.

"Except as I've been cuckolded something on the order of

five thousand times in forty years, I'd vanish from history like a tin can," said the professor. "No one remembers the beautiful Paris because of his taste in women, anymore than they'll remember Mrs. French here because she had a husband with a hot pussy, *or,*" the professor added speedily to forestall expressions of shock, "because she crossed paths this afternoon with a man who's been talking his head off since Christmas."

"Tell us what it was like on the mountain," Mrs. French instructed, her hands and head poised like glass, a soft glassy smile on her lips.

"If Menelaus had read the moderns," the professor continued, "he'd have used cyanide and rattraps. Why rely on honor if you're seven feet tall? You don't have to be Greek to know that Hercules bashed up his family and brained his lute master. I'm covered with welts from head to foot. I haven't known a moment of human affection since I looked out the kitchen window and saw Mr. Ashley Dan Marion standing, lean and pale, at the edge of the forest, with a pack on his back and a compass in his hand, trying to relocate the Appalachian Trail!"

Mrs. French's guests laughed appreciatively on all sides.

"By sunset, she had a hickory finger the size of a ball bat up his back-kitchen flue, and he," cried the professor, "trilling away like a little schoolgirl! She's all whiskeyed up and feeling happy, and just tips him over, and gives him a fine, quick go of it on the fender of her car! She just got a contract to wipe Bellows Falls off the map, and he's cuddling up to her all evening, filling her cup and simpering and blushing, you know, while giving me ugly cutting looks, and dusting a little here and there, and picking up newspapers, and straightening. He wouldn't eat my boiled cabbage, and insisted on showing me how to thread the bobbin on a machine that went out of manufacture the year Thomas Wyatt was born! Ashley Dan Marion! With his leek soup and wintergreen salads!"

"Tell us about the mountain," said someone. "About the giant woman and all."

"He's *telling* you about the mountain," said Mrs. French sternly.

"It isn't my fault," the professor continued, "if the ground-hog missed its shadow this winter, or, for that matter, that it went outdoors at all. There was plenty enough shadow in the hole, if you ask me. What kind of hootch is this?" The professor held up his wineglass to the light, then drained it. "We were born in another age, Mrs. Prudhomme and I. An era as old as civilization itself. We believed in the goodness of nature and man. We believed in death and resurrection. We revered the soil of the earth, as it contained, you see, the blood and sweat of last year's agony. We believed that. We believed that death refreshes life, and therefore is life. We were the children, Mrs. Prudhomme and I, of the old agricultural age. We adored Jesus. My father," he said, "adored Jesus, and so did his father, whose name was Victor. The barn was the temple, and the meadow the sacred grove, and that's how it had been since time immemorial. Mrs. Prudhomme could have been a Theban princess. I'm not saying she was happy. I'm not saying that. We were not conceived to be happy. Ours was a world of absolutes. There was always the serpent in the garden. All I'm saying is that Mrs. Prudhomme was the farmer's daughter unparagoned. And now," Homer Prudhomme added, "that world, of course, is gone."

"And so is Mrs. Prudhomme," someone observed softly.

"I lived to see the destruction of the garden," Professor Prudhomme persisted. "It appalls me to realize that. The long black furrow of the plowshare curving up from the primordial wilderness peters out here. In me," he said.

Motionless in her chair, Mrs. French regarded the professor with a voluptuous proprietary eye that smoldered like anthracite in her flawless, glasslike face. "Tell us," she encouraged him gently.

"Junior Ballou was dead in France, and I was driving south in the big black car that his grandpa had given him three years back on his seventeenth birthday, a twelve-cylinder 1911 Franklin, when I ran out of gas not fifty feet from her house. And to tell you the truth, I was thinking about the dear boy when I drove over the hill into Amherst. I was still wearing my overseas cap and my army brogans and trousers. I was twenty years old to the day, the seventh of June, 1920. I wasn't as handsome as Galahad, or as wise and knowing as the heroes of antiquity, but I was young and full of vim and ready to do some living. Junior died in a blazing June sunlight, and now," said the professor, "two years on, I was trudging up to the doorway of Mr. Emerson's slaughterhouse, swinging an empty red gas can. I'll never understand it. Junior must have been walking at my side in the sun, guiding my footsteps." He threw up his hands. "I had an augury! I had a premonition! Something uncanny, something providential!" he cried. "I knew she was in there! Tell me how I knew. If I live to be a thousand, I'll never understand it. They were inside, the two of them, father and daughter. He had a pig hoisted on a pulley, a massive sow, about eight hundred pounds, swinging in a kind of harness. In one hand he was clutching a fistful of knives and stickers, and was just readying himself to dispatch the poor brute by way of a solid thrust into its throat, when I came up to the door.

"The girl was standing back of him in the shadows, and she had turned, you see, and was staring at me. She had beautiful blackberry eyes and long black hair. She was wearing a pair of the old geezer's pants, runty pants that stopped at her calves, with her legs coming out of them skinny as a heron's. She was staring at me, in shock," he cried, "as though I, Homer Prudhomme, were the fulfillment of a strange and awful prophecy."

Professor Prudhomme's fingers floated up to his face. "I had barbed-wire scars from here to here. I had a broken incisor and a broken eyetooth. I was homely! I was battered!

She smiled! At me! A simple grinning farmboy from White River Junction. As though I were Parsifal himself. By four o'clock that afternoon, we were lying under a mower in the orchard. I," he said, "was looking up her crupper, and she was somewhere down aft of me, making dunking noises like stones dropping into a well. How I loved that girl!

"God, she was a gorgeous piece! To me, she was everything that America ever wanted to be. Florence Nightingale and Betsy Ross and Hester Prynne all rolled into one. You could have mashed my bones into a fine dust. You could have pulverized me. I was senseless and bodiless, pure spirit. I went down the two roads of her eyes like a pilgrim to the Holy Land. I lost myself in Priscilla Emerson. God was too good to me. I never deserved that woman. The fortune of it," the professor cried. "The solid good fortune."

Moments before dinner, Nigel French, the man of the house, made his first appearance of the day, coming languidly down the big plum-carpeted staircase, looking very slim and elegant in a suit of white sharkskin, with snowy white shoes, a lavender cravat, a lavender handkerchief, and lavender shoelaces. He was smoking a lavender cigarette. Mrs. French, his octogenarian lover and spouse, regarded him with dilating ink-colored eyes.

"*Going out on the town?*" she hissed at him under her breath, as Nigel sashayed past her, not looking at her but smiling archly and twirling the car keys.

"If there *was* a town!" he snapped, saucily.

"She gave me a copy of Whitman's *Leaves of Grass*. She said she would like to emulate in the flesh what that man of words had done in the spirit," said Professor Prudhomme. "She wanted

to marry first. She wanted the imprimatur. She wanted to be
certified! I was to get *inside* the soul of Whitman. I was to
divine his every meaning."

The professor forked a dripping chunk of pig's kidney into
his mouth, chewing busily and talking all the while.

"Oh, how I suffered and read, and read and suffered. She
said that if I failed with Whitman, she would put me on
Longfellow!"

He loosed a shriek of laughter.

"Book after book!" he cried. "God, I loved that girl! Paul
Poiret called her *La Sauvagesse*! She came at you like a toma-
hawk! She was taken up overnight by Molyneux, Paquin, the
Duchesse de Gramont.

"We," he said, "were living in a garret. We had a dog
named Ferdie. I was writing a book about the French poets."
The professor laughed heartily, and gulped down an entire
glass of water. "Why, I didn't know a poem from a crab apple!
I was twenty years old! I was a hick! She had more French
poets in that bed than I had in my bibliography. Ferdie had
met them all, too. One day she said to me, 'You know, Tup,
you ought to let Ferdie write that book, and you write a book
about something you know more about than he does!'"

"Isn't that the devil!" piped someone.

"I didn't learn to speak French," said the professor, "and
when we lived in Munich, I didn't learn your German. I
didn't need it. I loved my wife. Those were the days when
Mrs. Prudhomme and I were as happy as two meadowlarks.
I didn't even speak English!" The professor laughed with the
food showing in his mouth. "I didn't talk much at all. Mrs.
Prudhomme used to have an expression. 'Nouns ought to
verb,' she used to say, but she didn't mean that they had to
talk, you see. I was the living epitome of the Yankee farmboy.
I smiled, I brooded, I nodded, I shrugged. I read books. I kept
a journal. That was when I was memorizing old Walt for her,

from cover to cover. 'Just keep going as you're going,' she used to say. I recall her sitting on the edge of the bed in Munich, wearing a navy and white tweed skirt and a big white boating sweater, and looking like the Park Avenue college girls you used to see in later years in the Frauenkirche on Saturday afternoons—hatless, beautiful complexions, easygoing, that uniquely American look Europeans secretly both despised and admired in those days, a successful innocence, that quality of unsinning good fortune. She wanted to hear Walt, she said. She often asked me to chant him. If you live inside him, she said, with your whole heart, deep inside him, then he will have you, Tup, and you will have him, and you will have others, too. Now, walk back and forth, she said, just as Walt would have, and gesture handsomely, and chant me 'Marches now the war is over,' word for word, each one, as it was written to be done."

Professor Prudhomme laid down his fork and raised his two hands.

" 'As I sat alone by blue Ontario's shore,
     As I mused of these mighty days, and of peace
          returned, and the dead that return no more—'

"You see, she knew me better than I knew myself. One night there, at number 90 Schleissheimerstrasse, I had a bad dream. I woke up in Mrs. Prudhomme's arms. It was about Junior.

"I had gone back in my sleep, you see, back over the same terrain, with my heart beating like mad, and down the same grassy knoll we had lost the day before, and found him, floating there, facedown in the shallows, his helmet gone, his riflestock cracked in two. I was trembling like that!" The professor brandished his fists. "It was Junior, just as before, point for point, in the dreaming and the wakeful head. Point for point!" he cried. "The tiny blond hairs on the nape of his neck! We went to Miss Lyman's school together. I knew the back of his head as a baby knows its mother's breast. Mrs. Prudhomme was holding me in bed! I was shaking like a leaf. She said I was a born lover, a lover of man in all his grand and piteous ways. It would have to suffice me, she said, to know that if it had been me left behind in the retreat instead of Junior, that tonight, somewhere up in Vermont, he, Junior Ballou, would be sitting up in bed in *his* wife's arms, shaking like a leaf.

"You have to learn, Mrs. Prudhomme said, that there is never less than one, Tup, that zero is an abstraction. Light, she said, is not the absence of dark. Darkness is an abstraction, she said. There can only be light. I want you to think about that, she said. Nothingness is an abstraction, Tup, a human convenience, an invention."

"Of course," said Mrs. French, her sensuous voice husky with years, "I'm naturally put out by Nigel's manner, as you can imagine. If you hadn't come home when you did, I should very soon have had to take some extraordinary steps. He was quite attentive to instruction there for a while, but seems now to grow only more refractory as the autumn days go by. And if I accommodate him in his demands, which are egregious to the point of seeming unnatural, it only whets his appetite to test me further. He is quite spoiled, I'm afraid."

With the guests departed, Mrs. French served her distinguished friend a tall crystal cup of hot curdled milk laced with ale and sweetened with honey and nutmeg, offered him with her own hand. The glassy perfection of Mrs. French's delicate tapered fingers rose to the fine, brittle beauty of her wrist and forearm, which, in turn, led the eye to marvel upon the flawless neck, the perfect globe of her head, the matchless symmetry of her mannequin figure and slender legs, as she moved about him in a whisper of silks.

"I don't want to stifle his boyish spirits," she continued, as she slipped past the professor and led the way up the staircase, "but I am going to insist from here on out that he take everyone among us more seriously, not least of all himself. Youth fades," said Mrs. French. "Young men change. Virility suffers. Charm erodes."

At three that morning, Mr. Nigel French could be heard in the corridor outside his wife's boudoir, discussing his diminishing freedoms with her in a smart, snotty voice.

"And where am I to bed down? In some trough?"

"I'm very fatigued," Mrs. French replied, her ancient voice made more throaty still by the night air. "I would like to return to bed."

"Who are you enchanting tonight?" Nigel snapped back at her. "That rustic with the gold tooth? It isn't enough, Lucienne, just to take me to the big city on a shopping spree once a year, if I must be humiliated and ignored up here the rest of the time. To be put up in a fancy hotel for three or four nights, with a quick trip or two to the theater and museums, and a wardrobe of new clothes. I can't live like that, Lucienne. In six months, I'll be thirty, and then where shall I be? I am not like you!" he cried peevishly. "I don't have securities and trust funds and blue-ribbon animals to fall back on. I live by my looks!"

"What in the world is wrong with your looks?" said Mrs. French, as the argument persisted in the corridor.

"Which is something you can't understand! If you see something you like, you buy it!" he cried. "Let's be fair. Let's talk like human beings for a change. I," he said, "don't interest you anymore! You showed me off for a season or two to your friends and to your children and grandchildren, and to your attorneys and your boards of directors, at those silly luncheons, and then you were tired of me, just like that. As for our marriage contract," the man laughed thinly, "wasn't I the little fool? Whatever was in it for me? With those children and grandchildren and *their* children and grandchildren, and God knows who else, while I, your actual husband, will be expected to make do with some sort of pension, I suppose. I'll be reduced to begging!"

"Nigel!" Mrs. French flared up angrily.

"Oh, and I'll do it, too," he said, in a low, ironic voice. "What choice will I have but to suck up to your little great-grandchildren if I so much as need a pair of shoes or a roof over my head.

"Who's lying under your silver-and-canary bedquilts tonight?" Nigel demanded to know. "Henry David Thoreau? How long is he going to be with us this time? How long is he going to be nuzzling up to your snowy little panda? Because we all know what you can do with *that*. Well, he's not so fortunate as he thinks. Because he," Nigel shouted, "ran out on somebody who takes a dim view of that sort of thing!"

"You're being very difficult tonight," murmured Mrs. French.

Mr. French laughed nastily. "Everybody knows where he comes from! Everybody knows who he belongs to!" Mr. French was directing his anger now at the door of the boudoir. "Because I was with her tonight!"

"Nigel!" Mrs. French exclaimed hotly.

"Do you think I wasn't?" Mr. French was growing more abusive in tone. "Well, I was! And I'll tell you something else, while I'm at it. I *enjoyed myself,* Lucienne!"

"I forbid you to talk to me in this tone!"

"Some lovebirds play rough," he went on, "and I happen to like it. Does that surprise you? Some gals," he said, "don't do it with poems and secret possets. Some gals take it! Some gals," he shouted at the door in a fiery, provocative voice, "see what they like, and they take it! A certain local exterminator, for example!"

"If you persist in this maddening vein," Mrs. French was heard to reply, "I shall have our houseguest come out here and beat some sense into you."

"*Let him try it!*" Nigel shrieked at the door. "You just wait till that gal up on the mountain decides to come down here to settle accounts for herself. Then we'll see who's going to receive a good thrashing, won't we? *Won't we!*" he screamed.

The Flower of the Republic

. . .

Mrs. French set aside the crystal cup. "Just the thing for an Orphic bard," she said. She whispered past him in the darkened room, then whispered back again, and was lying on the silver-and-canary-striped coverlet, delicate as a figurine, her limbs shimmering like milk glass. "You may enter me now," Mrs. French said.

"It's the legacy of the garden," said the professor. "All of the fathers are venerable and all of the sons are vile, and the vile get to be venerable, not by growing old, but by spawning their own vile, who then lay them flat with clubs, fists, lead pipes, anything ready to hand. My own great-grandfather, Cyrus Prudhomme, cut down his father with a scythe, took half the old codger's leg away." When Homer Prudhomme laughed, his tongue lolled and sparkled in the candlelight. "Cyrus married a second time, a woman named Mrs. Cordelia Herbert, and his own sons cuckolded the poor devil one, two, three. Spent the winter of his days in an abandoned henhouse with his beard down to his knees!"

The professor was in high spirits. His words set off waves of sophisticated laughter among Mrs. French's circle of friends.

"Isn't that priceless?" said someone.

"Every man longs for his father's abasement," the professor said. "The Germans understand this better than most, you know. A German will begin to thrash his son the day he's born and will keep it up until he's too old to lift his arms. When Mrs. Prudhomme and I lived in Munich, I was treated to the sight of a sixty-six-year-old gentleman laying into his own son good and proper. It happened in our rooms, so I know what I'm talking about."

"Sounds edifying," said Mrs. French.

"More edifying for Reinhardt than for myself, I should think. Reinhardt was the peculiar duck who drank brandy from Mrs. Prudhomme's shoe one carnival evening, the same fellow she once shat upon for money when we were broke. The old father," Homer Prudhomme continued smoothly, "was great poo-bah of a place called Pfaffenhofen, an aristocrat-cum-industrialist named Georg Ritter von Scheubner-Harnisch. Georg took one look at Mrs. Prudhomme and exercised seignorial privileges that pushed the boy Reinhardt right out of the picture! We had been warned not to go to Munich. A bad year, a worthless currency—bread lines, the green police, brawls in the streets, shootings, you name it. Hell," the professor said, "Mrs. Prudhomme was picked up just like that! By the whole pointy-headed clan.

"What a sight they were! Reinhardt had a head shaped like an African termite mound, tall and pointy with a little thatch of red growth on the summit." Professor Prudhomme popped forward in a surge of amusement. "Picture him, stretched out in his evening clothes on the hotel room floor, with a towel tucked under his chin, his shiny black evening pumps sticking up, and she standing over him, straddling him, you see, drinking beer from a mug, bouncing up and down, flouncing out her skirts, *riding,* if you please. Pretend he wasn't *there,* he said, and she discharging! *Giddyap!*" The professor waved his fist in the air, and promptly fell into a fit of coughing and laughing.

"And that man thought himself a bigwig, this perfumed fop—pop-eyed, monocled, pumped full of cocaine, jabbering away in three languages. And for all that, he wasn't so extraordinary. Quite as typical a foppish piece of scum, according to Kandinsky, as many another to be found in that town in those days. Thousands just like him, Kandinsky said. Under every street corner.

"For one thing, you see," Professor Prudhomme lighted a

cigar, "the family money turned to paper. On top of that, a von Scheubner-Harnisch cousin, a magistrate in Landshut, turned up one morning in a public garden, shot and disemboweled. Now, to make matters worse, the old gentleman, Herr Georg himself, was sending picture postcards home to the family from the Elephant Hotel in Weimar showing him dancing the tango with a ravishing young black-haired beauty, whom they all recognized, believe me, because they'd seen her popping her way through the family firm on old Georg's arm more than once already, and looking damned snooty about it, too, throwing her twat around in a way that pleased the old fellow immensely, as it helped keep everyone in his place, you see. The family," Professor Prudhomme blew up a fine stream of cigar smoke, "saw the devil in it. Oh, yes, the perfect devil in it.

"Reinhardt, however, saw only me, sitting there by the window at number 90 Schleissheimerstrasse, with my pencils and green-covered notebooks. The funny part was he only came when he knew Mrs. Prudhomme wouldn't be there. He came Sunday mornings. He came carrying little bunches of violets or edelweiss, little nosegays of a strange mountain herb for Priscilla.

"For sheer blind Teutonic pigheadedness, the man was in a class by himself. Couldn't come when Mrs. Prudhomme might be there, since Herr Georg had put the kibosh on that, but every Sunday morning, about nine o'clock, there he would appear, stamping up the stairs in his embroidered knee stockings and leather shorts, jabbering away to himself. It took your breath away!"

"He must have loved her very much," observed the lady seated at the professor's left.

"I expect he wanted my help," the professor suggested. "Thought I might intercede for him. That I had some—some special drag with her, I suppose."

"Being her husband," said Mrs. French, unpleasantly.

"Exactly! But I didn't even talk, let alone conduct embassies to my wife on behalf of a pervert. I didn't say a word to him all that year. He would come in and park himself in a chair by the door, skinny bare legs sticking halfway across the room like a couple of two-by-fours waiting to be nailed up, and chatter his head off. I put the flowers in water. I gave him a glass of cherry brandy. I listened, I nodded, I sympathized. Reinhardt said that his life as a German was developing nicely, but that his life as Reinhardt the son of Georg Ritter von Scheubner-Harnisch was disappointing. As a German in good standing with certain factions of the right, he could easily, he said, have his father beaten to death some dark night and no one would be any the wiser, while as his father's son, however, he found himself susceptible to a secret nameless terror.

"The father, it seems, haunted the lad's dreams. Whenever Reinhardt talked about the old boy, I noticed he used the same words, and sometimes, too, he would pause, and *listen*. It was quite spooky, and yet," the professor added, "Reinhardt's fears were well grounded—because, as I said, I was there the Sunday morning when Georg came up the stairs with his cane."

Here the professor paused and removed his handsome linen jacket, put down his cigar, and set about the business of uncorking a bottle of wine.

"Oh, it was the devil to pay," he said. "You could feel it in the air. Tribulation was coming, and it was coming on two legs with a stick.

"I had a chinning bar in my closet. I was doing one-handed pull-ups at the time. I was quite a physical specimen in those days. In France, I had won the regimental foot race, running with fifty-pound sandbags on our shoulders, the strongest and fastest boy in three thousand. I was in the pink. Still am," he boasted, as he popped the cork and tilted the bottle to his glass.

"Mrs. Prudhomme didn't mind, so I had the chinning bar put up. Reinhardt's visits offered a good sustained opportunity for working out, because you couldn't read or write while he was in the room, or even think straight, as far as that goes, and I was up on the bar when I happened to glance out the doorway. And what do you suppose?" said the professor. "Mrs. Prudhomme was standing at the foot of the stairs! And someone was entering behind her! They were, you see, coming up the stairs!

"Priscilla came into the room first. She didn't look happy. She and Georg had had words. Georg came in behind her, looking pale—very stiff and correct, but pale. I tell you, my heart skipped. I was at the top of my exercise, with my chin propped on the crossbar. I just hung there, staring.

"Reinhardt had already flattened himself against the wall, his eyes shining like two minerals. Oh, yes, he was going to catch it now. Believe me, there was a thrashing in the air. You could feel it coming. And yet," the professor piped, and held out his cigar and wineglass in either hand, "it didn't materialize. They didn't even look at him! They didn't see him!

"Georg was complaining. He was saying, 'He's more than a responsibility, he's a burden,' and Mrs. Prudhomme, looking very girlish but grave, replied that there was still the alternative of shipping him back to school in Franconia and letting *them* handle the matter. They seemed," Homer Prudhomme suggested, "to be talking about someone who wasn't present, but were both so scrupulously oblivious of Reinhardt, as well as of myself, and of Reinhardt's terror and my own burning curiosity, that you couldn't help guessing that it *was* him they were talking about.

"Mrs. Prudhomme strode back and forth in front of the elderly gentleman, arguing softly, trying to put a reasonable face on matters, while he, Georg, appeared to be growing more furious by the minute. In any event, the old aristocrat cut a nifty figure, very handsomely got up in a long velvet coat and striped trousers. Had a flawless mustache and a cylinder hat and a cane with an ivory knob, and continually, while speaking, you see, he tapped the knob of the cane against his palm. Like this," Professor Prudhomme demonstrated, "saying to her in a thin, frightening voice, 'I will not be taken advantage of by a little hound who passes his time playing tricks behind our backs. By a despicable little pup!' "

"That does sound threatening," said one of the diners not yet heard from.

"Indeed," said the professor. " 'But he did promise,' Mrs. Prudhomme said. You see, as young as she was, Priscilla was being very grown-up and levelheaded in offering this person, this child, whoever it was, a second chance. 'He promised me,' she said. *'And,'* said Georg, 'may I ask when?' 'Why,' she thought about that a moment, 'just yesterday,' she said. 'Where?' said he, very softly, not believing. 'In his latest letter,' Mrs. Prudhomme replied. 'And may I see it, please?' Georg asked in that same musical, threatening voice.

"By this time," Professor Prudhomme explained, "I was becoming more interested in the drama taking place between Georg and Priscilla than I was in the really incredible situation surrounding it in reality! Reinhardt was dying a thousand deaths! He was in shock. Or I thought he was. His lips were white and bubbling. And they still didn't see him. Oh, they were so sure of themselves. They *didn't* see him!" the professor cried. "They didn't see anyone! They were as formal and detached as figures thrown onto a screen. They were conversing in *private*. They honestly were.

"Mrs. Prudhomme slung her houndstooth coat over a chair back and watched as the elegant old fellow held up the note she'd handed him and perused it with a slow wagging of his head. 'You see,' she said, 'he promised me.' But Georg Ritter von Scheubner-Harnisch was not convinced. He had something by the tail, you see. He had that sixth sense of the born authoritarian. You couldn't hoodwink him. Somewhere," said the professor, "the Kraut smelled a rat.

"He was quiet, though, for the longest time. He just stood there in the center of our little room, with his hands folded behind his back, gazing up at the ceiling, the stick swinging to and fro behind his knees. Mrs. Prudhomme seemed to have settled the question to her own satisfaction, and was going about the business that had brought them up there in the first place. She was changing clothes. Skimming about, peeling off her dress, opening and closing drawers, but keeping up all the while a cheerful patter about Europe, about Germany, about Bavaria, and after that about America, how the streetcars ran once every hour if you were lucky, and at one point, while she was putting on stockings, even launched into a comparison between the goose and the turkey, and of how one American turkey could satisfy the protein requirements of an entire family for a week, or a month, or God knows how long, I don't remember. What I do remember is Reinhardt, standing back flat to the wall, foaming at the lips, and breathing like this."

Professor Prudhomme drew a deep breath and held it for several seconds; then he let it out in a rush, dropped his head with feigned exhaustion, waited several seconds, and drew another deep breath.

"The life was going out of him. Of course, by then, I had come to realize that the fellow wasn't really there, and that it didn't matter. His existential condition, that is. No one was looking at him, and, truly, I wasn't, either. I," the professor said, "was watching that deadly, hypnotic stick—going back and forth, *back* and forth, *back* and forth, rhythmically, just like that, casting its spell, *back* and forth, until, lo and behold, it stopped!"

Homer Prudhomme sat up rigidly, his body tensed. "Even Mrs. Prudhomme noticed, and she was facing the other way. She felt it, you see. She turned to him. 'Sweetheart,' she said, 'what is it? You look frightful.' The stick with the big ivory knob was not moving in Georg's hands, and his eyes were shining like agate. 'I wish,' she said, 'you wouldn't let this matter spoil our Sunday outing. We've had it out,' she said, 'please let it be.' All the while she spoke, though, Reinhardt's father was staring at her in a most peculiar way, as if he were not looking *at* Priscilla, but trying instead to show her through the unbelievable intensity of his eyes that something else, something visible, even perhaps very nearby—perhaps," said the professor, "behind him—was amiss. Because Mrs. Prudhomme thereupon started to walk slowly toward the old gent, looking perplexed and casting her eyes everywhere about the room.

"Oh, I said to myself, they've got him now!" Professor Prudhomme laughed good-naturedly. "They know he's here. But whatever it was that had aroused the old man's suspicions escaped his young lady-friend. At one point, she even went to the window and looked out. As luck would have it, she didn't see Reinhardt, who seemed," said the professor, "to be standing right next to her. I surmised, however, that if Priscilla Prudhomme couldn't see him at a range of four feet, then neither could the father. I was right. It wasn't Reinhardt. Reinhardt," the professor pointed out, "was, for all intents and purposes, a phantom, as, for all intents and purposes, was I. No," Homer Prudhomme waved his cigar in the air, "it wasn't that. It was something else. After a moment or two, Georg fell to whistling a soft melody under his breath, the stick swinging back and forth again. His eyes, though, stayed fastened on Mrs. Prudhomme.

"It was then, just as I was beginning to despair somewhat myself, she saw it. Something *was* amiss. Either, you see, something was absent that was supposed to be there, or else something was there that ought to have been elsewhere. With just the slightest dip of his eyes, old Georg tipped her off. Mrs. Prudhomme snapped a quick look around behind her, toward the blanket chest by the door—for there, you see, peeping out of a crockery jar, was a delicate bouquet of edelweiss.

"We were all looking at it now. For Mrs. Prudhomme had clapped a hand to her mouth in a gesture of great amazement. Old Georg could be heard humming to himself and rocking on his toes. He was humming one of those oompah tunes popular with merry Alpine climbers, to which his cane kept a brisk accompaniment, cutting curlicues in the air behind his knees.

"Mrs. Prudhomme turned to him, looking altogether devastated. Her heart went out to him, you could tell. She walked toward Georg very slowly, shaking her head. It was a piteous scene. The old aristocrat was trying to keep up a brave front, you'll have to hand him that. 'Somebody's *been* here,' Georg sang out.

"Mrs. Prudhomme," the professor said, "went straight to Georg and put her arms around him. It was plain that she was not going to try any longer to make the way easy for somebody to continue to betray and distress Herr Georg. Whoever it was," snapped the professor sternly, "could depend no more on Mrs. Prudhomme's charitable offices. Not three minutes ago, in this very room, she had given this respected gentleman the most sterling assurances that someone, who was important to both of them, had given her *his* most solemn assurances about something of a very intimate nature, and here, with the words scarcely out of her mouth—here," the professor waved judicially, "was the little bouquet of flowers to make a mockery of it all. 'Of course, you were right, darling,' she said, 'and I was wrong and naïve and foolish, and I won't say another word about it. Treachery has to be dealt with.' Mrs. Prudhomme was sort of hugging the old boy, her head upon his breast, not wanting to speak, you know, but forcing herself by sheer willpower to do her duty and be brave now that reason had entered the picture.

"By then, I was pretty sharp as how to watch and follow

what was happening—at least as sophisticated as any of the early movie audiences. Movies were becoming popular then—that was 1922—and I was able to recognize that Reinhardt, standing panic-stricken against the wall, was actually portraying the horror that he *would* have felt had he been in the room. I mean to say, I had a good inkling by this time that it was Reinhardt they were talking about."

"It couldn't have been you," said Mrs. French, as she watched him from the head of the table with engrossed eyes.

"I knew it was Reinhardt," the professor went on, ignoring his octogenarian hostess, "because of certain clues furnished me by Georg and Priscilla, the little Nazi flowers in the crockery jar being not the least among them. Anyhow," he concluded, "Mrs. Prudhomme released Reinhardt's father and put on her shoes and skirt. But before leaving, she stopped in front of the old gentleman, and, while fitting her woolen tam atop her head, she spoke a few words of encouragement mingled with feminine admonition. 'Don't,' she said, 'please, Georg, *ever* allow him to lie to us again.'

"God in splinters!" the professor vociferated. "When Reinhardt heard that! He began sliding down the wall!

" 'Oh, have no concern about that!' old Georg shouted happily. 'I can guarantee it without equivocation. I'll teach the babe a thing or two! Yes, indeed. Oh, indeed, you may depend on it. Believe me, *liebchen,* I know just the remedy for a common alley cat, I certainly do,' and you could feel him just waxing himself into the proper mood for it, too," said the professor, pausing to drink, wiping his lips. "You really could. He was putting off that air of abandon that one feels when the resolution to act in a vigorous, even violent, way has put an end to inner stress. 'Why, I understand perfectly, my dear,' Georg said. 'After all, he hasn't lied only to me, now, has he? He's lied now even to you! For all his cock and bull! For all his *kauderwelsch* about love and devotion!' He spat these words

out. 'For all his talk of purity and idealism! His high princi-
ples. Why,' Georg said, 'why, he's nothing but a vulgar little
liar, now, isn't he? Oh, but have no concern, my pet,' he told
her in that oily voice. 'Old Europe has been boning up for
centuries on how to deal with liars.'

"I was tiring," said the professor, "not from the act of
clutching myself up to the chinning bar, you understand, for
it would no more have occurred to me to let myself down
than a moviegoer might be tempted to interfere with the cone
of light coming from the projection room in a movie house. I
was tiring," he explained, "from the stress of the drama! It
was a magnificent drama—I mean to say, classical in format—
Reinhardt made desolate by his father's appropriation of his
own true love, Reinhardt in love with the maiden who shared
his father's bed, Reinhardt wishing for his father's death,
Reinhardt haunted in dreams by the specter of his wrathful
father, and now, by his act of *devotion,* by the simple picking
of a handful of pretty white herbs, Reinhardt yielding himself
up to a blistering justice—and being compelled, mind you, to
witness the very working-out of his fate right before his eyes!
Why, it was rolled out for him like a bloody carpet!

"Mrs. Prudhomme took herself to the door, but you could
tell by the expression on her face that she was not fooled by
Georg's breezy manner. She knew that he was deeply wounded
and that the retribution he was about to exact could never
mend his heart. This was the moment in the drama, you see,
toward which everything that had so far happened had been
aiming. When Priscilla glanced back at Herr Georg from the
door, with the light of love," said Homer Prudhomme, "shining out of her face, one knew that this breathtakingly beautiful
woman from a faraway country had come to understand, in
the nick of time, that the old aristocrat had been right, that
he had shown his son to be a vulgar and deceitful scamp. Old
Europe had triumphed—if not forever, at least for today.

"Reinhardt, too, I believe, began to show signs of understanding. Until now, he had behaved like a blathering coward. He was, as I said, a little pop-eyed to begin with, but seeing Mrs. Prudhomme at the door, and that look on her face, knowing that she was lost to him forever, the lad became really quite ugly to behold. His eyes were starting from their sockets. He was shaking his head in horror, as if to say, 'Oh, no, please, no, don't leave me with him, don't go, please!' Of course, he wasn't saying anything, because he wasn't in a position to speak out, you understand. Reinhardt couldn't speak to the two of them any more than a character on celluloid might suddenly turn and begin to address extemporaneously a cinema audience. But one knew that the full weight of his maleficence was coming home to him now, for at any second this extraordinary young creature—the personification of mercy, of compassion, of New World charity, you might even say—was going to exit into the hall and leave him behind to be ground up alive.

" 'You just toddle along, my precious,' Herr Georg encouraged her; 'this little shindy will be over before it starts. Skip along now,' the old boy said, and he gave his stick a couple of bright twirls. 'Go down to the sweetshop, why don't you, and buy yourself a package of that American taffy you like so much.' He tipped her a wink. 'I'll just tidy up some unpleasant business up here,' he said, 'and be along in a jiffy.'

"Well, Mrs. Prudhomme made one final utterance before going, and in a small, penitential voice that summed up the crushing realization of her having been so childish and trusting of someone like Reinhardt, as well as expressing her deep happiness at having been forgiven so gracefully by the father. In fact, her words contained, I thought, every possible facet of humility, of modesty and demureness, even though," said Professor Prudhomme, "all she said was—'Thank you, Georg.'

"And that was it!" Homer Prudhomme cried. "She went out and closed the door quietly behind her. She was gone!

"Old Georg continued for a long moment to stare at the door. He stood in such a way as to be showing one profile to Reinhardt and one to me, much as a screen actor might dispose himself when directing his interest toward something in the background but not wishing to turn his back on the camera. Outdoors, at that same moment, the roof of a blue and white trolley went past below the window, trailing a blue spark, and that brought your eye up to Reinhardt. He had lost that wild, begging look. He had removed his monocle or eyeglasses, and stood with his head thrown back against the wall, his hand up to his forehead. He was crying his eyes out, but without making a peep. He had wet himself, too, of course. It came down from behind his lederhosen through the carrot-colored hair on his legs and trickled into the embroidered fold of his kneesocks. He wouldn't look at the father. Georg was not Priscilla Emerson Prudhomme, you understand. None of her New World spaciousness and optimism. Not by a far cry. No, Georg was another lug of the sow altogether," said the professor. "For all the fellow's impeccability, his Old Europe savoir faire, he was scion of a family whose pikemen paraded about the cobblestones of a hundred God-chidden villages with the heads of petty thieves and rascals on the points of their spears.

"I saw him turn—quick as a fiend!" cried the professor, "and dart his eyes in Reinhardt's direction. Mind you, that was the first time Reinhardt's presence in the room had been acknowledged. Mrs. Prudhomme's footsteps had faded on the stairs. The silence was palpable," Homer Prudhomme whispered. "Then, slowly, the old gent started forward in Reinhardt's direction—going softly, you see, on tiptoes, while slowly lifting his stick." Here the professor sat forward, gripping an imaginary cane above his head. "Like someone," he whispered, "creeping up on an unsuspecting rat. Easy—easy does it—easy now.

"As much as you knew what was coming to the lanky redhead, still," the professor exclaimed, "the sudden flash of the ivory-headed stick whirling downward and the sound of it connecting with Reinhardt's skull came as a shock—a thwack! that was as revolutionary as talking pictures. Like that!"

Again Homer Prudhomme demonstrated the blow with a vigorous overhand gesture. *"Thwack!"* he shouted.

"Reinhardt let out a yowl that could have been heard in every theater from Oberstdorf to the Zuider Zee even without your electronic amplifiers. After that, the old father laid into him with every ounce of strength he had. The cane was going like a piston. Even when Reinhardt lay flat out, looking immensely long on the floor, glasses broken, blood flowing, the old boy continued to beat him from head to foot. It was a caning meant to last the lad for a week or two.

"When the father was finished, he straightened his clothes, sponged his face with a silk handkerchief, and marched out of the room as composed as ever. I saw them from the window, Georg and Mrs. Prudhomme, as they crossed the street to Georg's car. Reinhardt left about an hour later, under his own power, after pressing some money on me for the 'use of the room.'

"When Mrs. Prudhomme came home that evening, I asked her if she'd heard the news." Here the professor shook his head in disbelief. "She said yes, she had, if I were talking about the drubbing the Greeks were taking from the Turks at Eskisehir and all the way back to Smyrna—it was a regular butchery, the papers said, and there was fear, too, even for the British position at Karnak."

Professor Prudhomme whooped with laughter.

"I told her I was talking about Reinhardt and his father! 'Oh, *those* two,' she said. 'Don't believe everything you hear about them.'"

Homer Prudhomme showed everyone an incredulous expression. "Isn't that the dickens? That was how cinema came to Europe. Christ, even *I* had thought it was real."

"I have always been fascinated by time," said Mrs. French. She was sitting opposite him, trim and lustrous, in the dove-gray interior of her limousine, as the trees rolled past the tinted windows in an amber haze. She was lotioning her aged hands. "Our perception of things must always be that of something small locked up inside something big. That's why we mortals take a humble view of ourselves against the great cosmos out there. To begin to appreciate the reverse scale of things, of constellations of worlds encompassing smaller worlds, and worlds within those worlds, and of more and ever smaller worlds, receding to infinity, why," she breathed softly, "we should have to turn ourselves inside out. It is only because we grow tall that our flowers do not close at dawn, or our falling stars race contrarily to achieve the mystery of their origins."

Mrs. French capped her lotion bottle. "Nigel," she said, "requires instruction in these regards. He's such a bad child. He is just beginning now to appreciate how time and world can conspire to bring one to one's knees. I told him only this morning to put aside croquet for a while and bury himself in his cookbooks. The child actually listened!"

Professor Prudhomme's brain was trying to situate itself in time and place. Mrs. French's silk stockings squeaked as she crossed her legs.

"I have a bee in my bonnet that tells me," Mrs. French

continued, as she put up her lotion bottle, "that you might be just the medicine he needs. Perhaps you could take him aside," she said. "Explain to him that we're really quite displeased with him, you and I, and touch, too, Homer, while you're at it, on the subject of hygiene. He's too old for carousing with milkmaids. Don't be afraid to lecture him," she said. "Tell him how I feel about disease."

Silver points danced in the irises of Mrs. French's eyes, as she turned toward and away from Homer Prudhomme while speaking.

"The trouble with Nigel," she said, "is he's not young enough to have stars in his eyes anymore nor old enough to be seriously frightened by matters of time and death. How long he'll be content to remain in the kitchen, currying chicken and coring winter apples, is as perplexing to me as the riddle of the Sphinx. But I have been so impatient with him sometimes that I believe truly I could have trampled him to death on one of the bridle paths. Do you recall last year, before you went away, when you and I were dining at the Coolidge, the night Leon and his wife were called away, how very upset I was when Nigel forced himself into the room for money, and you could actually *see* that vulgar strumpet of his in her scarlet blouse smirking in the lobby. That's just the sort of impertinence I'm talking about."

While listening, Professor Prudhomme examined the perfect crease of his handsome summer trousers, and stole a peek at his silk hose and garters.

"Otherwise," she said, "although I am hesitant to give it a name, I am afraid that our loose-moraled Mr. French may find himself in a pickle not so different from what you experienced yourself years back, when you were left in the lurch. Think on it. I know it is an imposition—but, either way, I shall continue to concern myself with your welfare, and there's no reason why we shouldn't continue, you and I, to be an item, socially. Take him out for a walk!" she exclaimed, with theatrical heartiness. "Take him into the garden, or into the tool house, or even out back by the golf green, and tell the boy what's what! I am not squeamish." She regarded the professor candidly from beneath long lashes. "I am not a romantic," she said. "I know what a person sometimes needs."

Abruptly, Mrs. French leaned and tapped with her cigarette lighter on the glass partition. "William, slow the car, please. Look, Homer, where we are! The Hollis Point bridge! The exact spot where we crossed by horseback the afternoon I spirited you away!" Mrs. French spoke these words with pride. "What a favorable sign."

While Mrs. French gazed down at the turbulent stream thrashing among cattails beneath the bridge, Professor Prudhomme fell to studying his salmon and cinnamon necktie, squeezing the nubby shantung between his fingers. He had never seen it before. He was wearing spectator shoes, also, and a black onyx ring with a diamond in it.

Mr. French was, in fact, showing gray, but only in daylight, and only then at the edges of his carefully coiffed hair. By candlelight, he was flawless.

"If you ask me," he said, "you and Dad ought to slip down to Cuernavaca this winter. You have property there, and you could motor up to the city weekends."

"Homer and I have done quite enough traveling, thank you," said Mrs. French, as she addressed her dinner. Outside the panoramic window, a falling snow blew sidewise through the spotlighted birch trees. "Whenever Nigel wishes to divert attention from another of his culinary masterworks, he invariably brings up travel," she said, "as though Homer and I were a couple of Canada geese with nothing better to do than nibble on a plate of wild rice and go winging down to the tropics!" Her retort incited a gay response from her table. "When he calls Homer 'Dad,' you may be sure he has created something toothsome, so we must continue to make him a great show of approval." Mrs. French smiled indulgently upon Nigel, the glow of the candles lending her features and flesh a special translucence. She sat with her delicate hands upraised, her black smoldering gaze passing like a beacon from face to face. The professor, at the foot of the table, was busily spooning up marron glacé.

"What do you think, Homer?" she inquired. "Where do you suppose the fashionable set are wintering this year?"

"Is it winter?" the professor said, causing a second wave of gay laughter. "I spent my winters alone. The only time I didn't, I was sorry. When you peek in windows, you get what you deserve. Life requires a little faith. When I married Mrs. Prudhomme, she was as lithe and youthful as Mrs. French!"

"Bravo!" came a rapid response.

"Her hair was as black, her eyes were as black, and her leg was as trim. Between the fall of Poland and the bombing of Hiroshima, she put on one hundred and eighty pounds."

"Dad," said Nigel, "hasn't stopped talking in about seven years. But *I* stopped listening the first week."

Professor Prudhomme waved his spoon at Mr. French in disgust. "He," he said, "requires documentary evidence that he was a full-term baby!"

Not loath to take up the role of the professor's putative son, Nigel closed the top of a casserole and came to the table. The professor saw not, however, the dapper, dissolute Nigel French, but a smiling young fellow in military whites, with brilliant shoes and a blond flattop.

"To him," the professor cried, "the past is the rumble of Hannibal's horse crushing the Roman salient! That's not history," he cried angrily. "History is the part that *doesn't* change!"

Nigel looked to the others with a smirk, then to the professor. "What am I to make of *that?*" he snapped, and his eyes widened and narrowed to slits.

"That was me you saw in the multitude! That was me you saw in the mass! Coming up Broadway with my regiment, home from the war fields. That was me printed up in the news photos! A face on parade!" he cried. "A fetus of the twentieth century! A woodchuck from White River Junction!"

Nigel continued to regard Homer Prudhomme with equanimity, but turned now to Mrs. French, who, after a thoughtful pause, brought down her eyelids to signify her permission for her spouse to make a suitable reply.

"It's beyond me," the professor went on, "how a boy of twenty Christmases can count himself worthy of pity just because his mother took a trip!"

"When people go on a trip," Nigel lashed back in sudden heat, "they don't take the curtain rods and doorknobs!" Nigel let that remark sink in. "They don't take the mailbox!" His eye riveted itself with hatred upon the professor. "Mommy," he spat out the word, "took every needle and thread in the place! She took last winter's newspapers! She took the lawnmower and the coal hod! She took the Ball fruit jars!" Nigel leaned, and placed his fists on the table. "I was cut out, and you know it!"

"You were cut out because you wouldn't *come* out!"

"I was cut out," said Nigel, "just as Lucinda was cut out."

"What verisimilitude," said one of Mrs. French's guests.

"He was a full-term baby!" the professor waved elaborately at Mr. French. "And then some! The son of a bitch was huge!"

Nigel French looked away with contempt. "Lucienne feeds them mast, and they grovel about in their own swill, hoping just to discover what day of the *week* it is! Or how many eggs there are in a dozen!"

"Nigel!" Mrs. French scolded.

"Mother," Nigel explained to the others, "was wearing a yellow oil-slicker that spring, and every time someone up north spotted a sprig of forsythia, they would go *running,*" he said, "to a telephone!"

Everyone laughed over that, even Mrs. French herself, as Mr. French turned and went back to toying with his casserole.

"The morning we were married," Professor Prudhomme said, "Peleg waved from the hill. Old Marjorie kissed Priscilla's hands. When we left Amherst, Dana was hiding behind a tree. She was that beautiful, I say! A miracle in white! And her first imbroglio wasn't seventy-two hours off. We were sailing for France. He came aboard at Halifax! He was as big as that!" The professor threw out his arms.

"Lucienne!" Nigel protested.

"The man was immense! Fatter than Honoré de Balzac! Oh, yes, women like beefy men. The fat red fist pounding on waxed teak! They like it! Well, the man took your breath away. They were coming together in the companionway, coming back from the ballroom. I never saw anything to match it! He could have been one of her daddy's own Tamworth porkers! Everything about him! The hams, the loins, the jowls, the snout! You would not have thought human sperm could work that way. The pink leathery skin," he cried, "the bristles, the scrunched-up pig eyes! Even down to the blue ribbon in his lapel! Puti!" cried Professor Prudhomme. "A bona fide baron no less. I could've reached out and touched them. They were coming right at me. Mrs. Prudhomme was in furs and gray velvet, with a little gray velvet cloche shaped like dog's ears atop her head, and with her gloved hands up like paws. She was that sleek! She didn't *affect* not to see me. She didn't see me! Her nose was in the air, her hindquarters trembling all over, his fat red hand on her buttock. She was his whippet, his *windhund!* They weren't aboard an ocean liner. They were at the race course. He had her papers in his pocket. She was domesticated, don't you understand! She was primed. She belonged. *She was ready to run!*" he hollered.

Nigel brought down a big serving fork with a clatter. "I don't have to listen to this!"

"No wonder he took her from behind! She was in the devil's own pens. Hers was no honeymoon on stilts, believe me. Mrs. Prudhomme was the undergroundling who closed the book on the subject. Oh, yes, they knew her in the vales of Enna, you know, where she with wicker ark did come, to kiss and bear the cowslips home. They knew her! They knew her in the kindergarten on West Street, coming to the schoolhouse on a September morning in her royal-blue jumper and patent-leather shoes. She came with Mrs. Benvenwyn. They cut tulips out of paper. They sang 'Joy to the World.' That was in the upper air, in the wealds of light. That," he said, "was the day before yesterday. But not in your world or mine. She hadn't even unlocked her trousseau yet, and here she was, balancing the porcine belly on her forehead, servicing an empire! But *I* was the *ignis fatuus*. They weren't blind! I'm talking about regions where solids," he said, "constitute a charming diversion, a dream in the night, a ghost story."

Mrs. French, opposite him, was not sitting in her chair any longer, but had receded to her puffy yellow-and-silver bed. The windows were thrown wide on a matchless summer night.

"I," the professor set his fingertips lightly to his breast, "can be deceived. There is a synapse between knowing and not knowing. There is a lull between the transit of the moon and the rush of the lunar tide."

"And I," Mr. French was complaining bitterly from somewhere behind him, "am supposed to be repressing all of this, I suppose."

"I'm talking about the sacred conjugant! I'm talking about flesh." Professor Prudhomme balled his fists. "I'm talking about gristle!"

"I'm supposed to be up in my bed, worrying myself sick about the little gingerbread man, while you and Mom are really laying to it in there!" Mr. French was in the hallway, shaking the closed door. "What did you buy me for Christmas?" he screamed acidly. "Another chemistry set? Because if you think I'm going to blow myself up, Camerado, you have another thought coming to you! I know when I'm being made a little fool of!" He rapped sharply on the door. "Are you listening?" he shrieked.

"Come to bed, Homer," said Mrs. French, her snowy pelt shimmering in the summer moon as she rearranged her glass-like legs upon the counterpane.

"She was as lovely as you," said the professor. "I was her Alpha Centauri, the nearest of the far. She told me so. Honor me, and I will love you for time and eternity, she said."

"Put out your cigarette," said Mrs. French, her big, loving, oil-colored eyes fastened obsessively upon him.

"*Are you listening?*" Nigel shrieked. "I'll stay here all night if I have to!"

Professor Prudhomme extinguished his turquoise cigarette. Mrs. French wound her dainty arms about his back, her fingertips pressing at his spine, her perfect lips parted. She whispered, "My adorable one."

At twilight, Mr. French threw down his croquet mallet in a fit of pique and strode angrily up to the house, kicking a big orange-striped wooden ball out of the way as he went. He was incensed at the approach toward Mrs. French's house of a certain notorious Miss Thomas, an athletic blond archer, a young Diana of the neighborhood, fabled thereabouts for once having nailed the tail of Mr. French's lavender cardigan to the drawing-room wainscoting with an arrow she'd let off without warning. Miss Thomas came silently in silver sandals over the moon-silvered grass, with bow and quiver and feathered cap, her two silver hounds running smoothly before her, to report the apparition of "a veritable Omphale," she said, down by the road.

The croquet players turned as one, and gazed out through the dewy twilight, past the topiary shrubs, to see the distant figure of a Brobdingnagian woman standing, with thongs about her legs, her arms akimbo, by the open door of her Rocket 88.

He could feel the cold air blowing down from the window and knew it was snowing. He could hear the snow. Someone was standing over him. It was Ashley Dan Marion, his red-gold hair shining.

"It's Dad," he was saying. "He's awake."

Pansy Truax was looking over Ashley Dan's shoulder, her pretty moonlike face blooming, her pink arm encircling his waist, as she fondled Ashley Dan openly.

"*I* would leave him in the forest," said Ashley Dan.

"Give him one of my nightgowns," she said, "and a belt."

"I'd like to give him a belt!" said Ashley Dan, and his eyes narrowed. "After all these years! The old coot! Grubbing for mushrooms like a wild animal."

"Give him a bowl of hot milk," Pansy said.

Ashley Dan was talking to himself in the kitchen, banging the pots about and opening and closing cabinet doors.

"I said bring Prudy his milk!" Pansy called from the parlor now as the birchwood settee squeaked underneath her weight. "And put some bread in it!"

"Every time he goes traipsing off," Ashley Dan was complaining in a pinched, monotonous voice amid a rattling of china, "I can only pray he'll be lost for good. Good grief, just the cigar smoke!"

"There won't be any more cigar smoking," Pansy Traux

announced for everyone to hear. She could be heard shaking out her newspaper. Professor Prudhomme was wide awake, listening keenly.

"If it were up to me," Ashley Dan said, as he went about his work, "I would know what to do with him. *And* with his talk, talk, talk."

"You all talk," Pansy said.

"The man doesn't make a lick of sense, if you ask me," Ashley Dan muttered. "To me, he's just another mouth to feed. I'd put him out in the wind. I find it hard to believe that I was once jealous of a smelly old vagrant like that."

Ashley Dan went past the doorway in a blue apron, carrying a platter of eggs and a pot of coffee. A splinter of the morning sun ignited his red-gold hair. "Talk, talk, talk. But it's impossible for me to imagine the two of you ever having had anything in common really to talk about. I chatter away, but I try to make sense. My goodness, look at that snow," Ashley Dan exclaimed. "At least, it will give me a chance to wear the new boots you bought me. That's a consolation," he raised his voice to declare. "I'm going to wear my green serge trousers, because they're warm and they look nice, with my Black Watch tartan shirt and my cable pullover, the one I wore to the agricultural fair in Acworth the day you won the maple syrup. That's my lucky sweater."

Twice more Ashley Dan Marion went by in the doorway carrying teacups and plates and a covered dish. Returning, he paused to fix Professor Prudhomme with a menacing look.

"Have you given Prudy his bowl of milk?" Pansy Traux asked, after an interval.

"Not *yet*," Ashley Dan snapped from the kitchen. "I only have two hands."

He could then be heard setting down a utensil with a clink, this followed by a pause of such duration as to give notice of his pique. A full minute later, Ashley Dan came spinning into the room with a bowl of steaming milk and planted it noisily next to Professor Prudhomme's bed while showing the old educator a set of malevolent bottle-green eyes. He had untied his apron, and was folding it carefully in sections. "If I catch you among my things this time," Ashley Dan whispered evilly, "I'll scratch your eyes out!"

"I know what a fetlock is," said Professor Prudhomme, "and I know a petcock. I know a turkey cock from a bucksaw and how far it is from Poppasquash to Pottawoone, but if you could have seen me coming down the rue des Ecoles from the Pantheon and out past the crowded cafes, with Mrs. Prudhomme at my side clicking along a mile a minute, with her armlets and bracelets and chokers flashing, with her veils and ostrich plumes trembling, and I at her side, I in my blue coveralls and rubber-bottomed duck boots!—and heard the din go up from a hundred tables at the sight of us—the shouts and the catcalls and the hat waving!—*La chasseuse des bisons!*—*Perséphone des Enfers!*—I swear to Jesus, I was the laughingstock of Europe! A woodcutter from the hills of Vermont!

"But that was the beauty of it! The holy disparity! I loved my wife! I adored my wife! I'd've given my life for her at the drop of a hat. I was an innocent! I knew the meaning of hope. I knew the meaning of faith. To lie at night in that woman's arms was like dropping off to sleep in the most original of all embraces, in the oneness of something so ancient as to make the lifetime of God Himself seem but the flaring up of a match. When Mrs. Prudhomme lost Lucinda, I held her in my arms, and we must have dropped through space for an eternity."

Professor Prudhomme listened carefully. He could hear the swish of a tail and the starting up of an automobile engine. He didn't know where he had got them, but he was wearing spectacles, and with them on could discern the sudden green eruption of a firefly. In the dusklight framed by the privy door, the fields beyond receded into blackness. The car went away.

Bye and bye, he heard footfalls on the grass.

Professor Prudhomme was sitting on the wooden seat, looking up, when a figure materialized in the doorway, just a silhouette, a blaze of golden hair, and something in hand of an ominous nature, a bat or club.

An instant later, the professor was dealt a cracking blow on the head, then a second blow to the face, a blow that broke off a tooth and sent him sprawling on the sodden outhouse floor. He was belabored then from head to foot, each blow accompanied by a shriek that pierced the summer dark like the cry of a bobcat. One of the more viciously aimed blows shattered his eyeglasses and knocked them flying.

PART THREE

The Meadows of Asphodel

꧁ "Only a fool would weep after so many years. Her name was Lucinda. She lived about as long as it takes to drink a cup of coffee."

His hair fluffed up in the wind, Professor Prudhomme stood beneath the poised hoof of Ethan Allen's bronze horse, the shadow yawning eastward in the blue April afternoon.

"She came up from a darkness as old and unfathomable as Old Chaos itself, gulped a few lungfuls of hospital air, and sank back into darkness. She was my daughter," he said. "I touched her with my fingers, a little parcel of flesh, breathing fast, mouth open, pulling for air.

"Do you know," Professor Prudhomme said, "on many a lonely night, while sitting under lamplight, with my papers or a book, I have felt her come stealing to life beside me. In that way, I watched her grow. She was not," he said, "the invisible guest at dinner. She was not the ghost in the empty chair. Hers was the place at table that is never set, the bed in the room that was never laid down. I saw her in the shadow of the tree outside my window, I saw her in the shadow of my bookcase, or here," he said, extending his hand palm downward, "in the shadow of my hand."

"You're an honest man," spoke a voice.

"Call me a charlatan," Homer Prudhomme said. "Call me a quack. When she fell out of the sunlight, when she fell tumbling back through the volumes of darkness, I held her hand. I held on. I was supposed to. I had a belief that went beyond believing. I had a love that went beyond all that. I was her father."

"I'll tell you a story," he said. "When Eben Whitaker, the Star-Route carrier, pumped his Klaxon and whipped up the horses, and his green-and-blue mail coach rolled away in spangles of sunlight, with Aunt Daphne perched on the seat beside him, her flaxen hair bright as the sun, it was as though morningtide itself had come to an end. She was twenty-nine years old. She had no face at all, just a waxen oval of scar tissue—that," he said, "and a real mask, a papier-mâché contrivance on a stick, a fright in itself, with two narrow eye-slits, that Daphne raised up whenever anyone chanced by. Daphne of the golden tresses. Daphne the deep-bosomed, the glory of the Memphremagog, loveless and childless, spent seven years in my father's house, and then vanished like a sunbeam.

"One night that summer, a man named Ozra Browning was dragged to his death by runaway horses on the road to Pomfret, and the very next day, Daisy, who was Ozra's wife, found a black satin dancing pump in her grain bin. Daisy said it was Daphne's pump. She remembered Daphne! She remembered her dancing the Portland fancy at the Grange Hall, she said, back in ninety-nine, when Daphne was a stranger in White River Junction, not to say, the toast of the season! Now they said she was a witch. Daisy Browning stood up in church and called her that—a sorceress, a devil, a witch. She went out at night, she said. When Daphne heard," said the professor, his voice dropping to a whisper, "her heart turned to vapor on the spot. She was terrified. She turned our house upside down, and, God spare her," he said, "found only one pump!

"They fed her to the gods. Pelops got a new ivory shoulder,

Daphne got a papier-mâché face. They wanted her heart
Beulah Rivers saw a woman in white with long blond hair
dancing with a ghost baby at twilight by Harley Pond. It just
got going. No one could stop it. Daphne Otis was a solitary.
She drank sarsaparilla by the quart. She lived in veils. She
floated outdoors, and floated back. She trembled like an aspen.

"Father," he said, "walked with her down the road beneath
the golden chestnut trees. She took his arm. Father was in
black. Daphne's hair was as yellow as August itself. Ida, my
mother, was crying in the house, because of what Father was
telling Daphne, or just because he was telling her something,
or because they were walking in gold, I suppose, or maybe it
was because Daphne would be leaving now, after years together
under the one roof. Or maybe it was not that at all. Ida cried
the whole year. That was the year we lost my sister. Maybe,
too, Ida had got used to Daphne's austere regency. Maybe she
reveled in the shadows. Maybe Father crept to Daphne's room
at night. Maybe he did. I never knew.

"Now," he said, "the Star-Route man was coming. His
Klaxon sounded like a shot through the trees! And the drum-
ming of the hooves on the planks of the bridge exploding like
gunfire! That was Eben Whitaker, the Star-Route carrier,
coming like the devil in a cyclone of leaves! Daphne was
waiting. Stood," he said, "with her traveling bag standing
beside her in the gravel. Sometimes you'd hear Mr. Whitaker's
whip cracking even before he came into view. 'Hee-up-theah!'
and a *crack*, like that!

"Father watched as Daphne climbed aboard and settled
herself atop the high seat. Eben put up her suitcase. The
horses," he said, "tossed their heads, their eyes on fire. They
stamped, chewed at the bit, just itching to fly! Up went the
whip, like a snake, with a whistle and a *crack*! and exploding
horses left Father standing there, by himself, under the chestnut trees, with the leaves twinkling down.

"Daphne," Professor Prudhomme said, "was gone."

. . .

"Letters went back and forth between White River and Lake Memphremagog. My father grew sick with worry. Up north, the Otis family were bereft. They tried to retrace Daphne's steps. Father wasn't much help. He didn't know. He worried, he languished, he suffered. He grew careless of his farmwork; a lassitude came over him. My mother, who was Daphne's sister, was torn by feelings of remorse, as well, partly, I suppose, for the relief she felt over the removal at last of the scarred remains of the once idyllic man-woman love that she, Ida, had shared with my father—the old paradise," said Professor Prudhomme, "the one that lasts for an hour. Somewhere up around Thetford, Daphne Otis had missed a train. She was gone. Just like that. She sank into the earth, into the shadows of old New England, and it swallowed her up."

Professor Prudhomme was leaning in at the ticket window, addressing the bowed head of the Vermont Central night man. The station was empty, the street outdoors silent.

"She was an outcast," the professor explained, "a pariah. Mankind was finished with her. Daphne had entered the labyrinth. Whether she saved her soul or not, I don't know, or even if she had one left in her to save. But she kept herself alive. She kept flesh to bone! That's the trick, you know. Any donkey can save his soul."

The night man's head shone like an onion as he bent forward, toting up a column of figures with a worn pencil stub. Auto headlights played across the station windows.

"St. Theresa had a roof over her head," said the professor. "Francis of Assisi got free lunch. He had a warm bed. It takes three hots and a cot just to think about God, let alone work up a conversation with Him. It takes bread, cheese, berries, veal, olives. Christ, man, it takes something to eat!

"In Burlington, Daphne lived in a doorway for a week! She walked in thunder and rain," he said, "from Essex Junction to Belvidere. Her flesh was going, her sight was going. She was hungry. She was ridiculed by children, chased by dogs! She walked east, half out of her wits. At Eden Mills, she turned back. She went south to the Lamoille, and on west again to Waterville and Fairfax. The woman was going in circles! She was only thirty miles from home, but light years away from the mirror on the wall. Her coat was torn, her suitcase gone, her shoes worn to a sliver. On a morning in November, Daphne Otis was standing on the cobbles of an icy side street in Enosburg Falls, swathed in veils, wavering on her legs, staring up at a faded pink door, a derelict door, a portal at the end of the road. Her travail—her exhaustion, her hunger, her despair—was coming to an end. She raised a gloved hand and knocked. There was a stirring within, then silence, another stirring. She listened. At last," said the professor, "the door opened. Just that much," he made a space between thumb and forefinger, "and an eye appeared, wet and lustrous as a clam."

The night man looked up, as Homer Prudhomme showed him an illustrative blue eye.

"It belonged," he said, "to a penurious little Yankee by the name of Mr. Charles Longbottom, who lived there, like a recluse, on the ground floor of a bankrupt jute factory. And that was the form of Daphne's redemption. Mr. Longbottom peeped out the door that icy dawn and saw the lean, honey-haired lady in veils shivering in the wind, her jaw to one side, her gray eyes big as her stomach and crazed with a burning light. The pink door opened, and Daphne Otis glided forward amid a commotion of veils and frozen clothing, stepped across the little fellow's threshold without so much as a word or a breath or a sign of salutation—and vanished from sight for years and years.

"That's how it happens," said the professor. "There is a door in the wilderness! To him, you see, the woman was a walking saint! He worshipped her. He was crazy about her!

"Daphne took over a small upstairs room that overlooked a polluted canal covered with green and yellow weeds and industrial scum. She had four walls! A room of her own! She had a stove!" Homer Prudhomme cried. "A deal dresser, a bed, a table, a chair!

"Charles fell over himself ministering to her needs, fixing her meals, and attending to her laundry. He came and went on that rickety staircase with the devotion of a holy acolyte. Picture him," the professor said, "this man in his threadbare black suit, with his black tie and celluloid collar shining like a corpse, bringing the woman her firewood, her supper, her soaps, her bromo quinine, bringing down her dishes, her refuse, her chamber pot. He had a reason to live! A purpose in life. Daphne, remember, was in her prime. The man knew that! He had intimations! How could he not? He saw her hands, her throat, her ankle! The lift of her head, the beauty of her carriage, her waist, her bosom! You understand, he was a washed-out merchant, a destitute bachelor, a failure! For him, that icy dawn in 1907 was more sacred than Easter Sunday. He wasn't alone, after all. He wasn't forgotten. He was saved!"

Just as Professor Prudhomme was throwing his arms wide for emphasis, the station door opened and a big woman marched in. She was followed by a slender golden-haired man. The big woman, who was nearly white-haired, carried the luggage. She wore a Mackinaw coat and heavy-duty boots; the man trailing behind her bore a smiling, simpering expression on his lips, and walked with a delicate, if showy, movement of his lower body. The professor stood stock-still, and stared at the big woman as she strode boldly to the window of the night man and demanded two tickets for Niagara Falls. When she said Niagara Falls, her slim, golden-haired companion blushed swiftly and darted a smile of polite self-effacement in the direction of the startled educator.

"I want something clean," the big woman spoke up in a powerful voice. "Something clean and comfortable. My little friend here doesn't want to sleep on a bed of pain, and neither do I. I want a soft mattress and no vermin." The big woman withdrew her wallet. Her companion edged in close to her to watch with interest through the brass grille as the Vermont Central man busied himself with the transaction. The big woman took out a white, long-stemmed pipe, and knocked the bowl carelessly against her palm.

"I guess you know why we're going to Niagara!" she announced, her eye falling on Homer Prudhomme as she turned away from the man in the cage. "Mister," she shouted, "if you've got any ideas about boarding that Midnight Special, put them right out of your mind!"

Tickets in hand, the big woman collected her luggage and started for the door, her companion pressing against her and subtly urging her on, lest she embarrass him further with her rough talk.

"We'll get us a brew," the big woman declared, shouldering her way through the street door with her bridegroom following in her wake.

The professor watched them go.

Outdoors, there were no lights. The roadway was dark. The houses had become trees, the moon shining through them. The station house behind him was dark and silent.

"You can't blame Mr. Longbottom," he said. "By Christmas, he hadn't a thought in his mind but to fuss over Aunt Daphne. A time would come when Mr. Charles Longbottom hadn't one thing to do in this world but sit at the foot of the stairs in that jute mill of his and wait breathlessly for that grand, grand woman upstairs to knock on the floor for him with her stick. He fetched up her newspapers. He went back and forth to the post office. He brought her her vanilla wafers and her Canada mints, brewed her tea, soft-boiled her eggs. His hand shook in her presence! He didn't even dare look at her! That mask!" said the professor. "It was like the face of God! Longbottom's voice failed him in her presence. His heart contracted. Remember," Homer Prudhomme said, "Charles had never seen her smile, never a sign of favor, of approval, of anything! Just the smooth plaster face installed before him in the sunless air of that upstairs room, that ghastly mask with the eye-slits and the beautiful gray eyes sparkling inside them. And Daphne all that while busily writing, you see. Writing, writing, writing, establishing a journal of her days in Hell. The *Enosburg Day Book* it was called. I've seen the thing with my own two eyes!

"When that woman came down from that room on an autumn afternoon in 1927—actually crossed the threshold and descended the rickety steps to ground level—after twenty years!—seven thousand days and nights!—all that was left behind was her day book. A massive tome, thousands and thousands of pages, each filled from top to bottom in Daphne's tiny, almost indecipherable hand. That book," said the professor, "became the bible and centerpiece of the shrine of that oppressive little room, standing open there on the deal table, with the gray daylight throwing a hallowed glow over the black and red ink. And the language! Great God, I tell you, it was beyond belief."

Professor Prudhomme gazed up in the darkness to the ceiling, reciting, as from memory, in a rolling orotund voice:

" *'And the blue soul spaketh to the black these words, saying, "Yea, I have dwelt like the light of evening softly upon Her, and I have come away thrice and returneth thrice, and cometh away even as many times again,"' and to these words the black soul, as heretofore, gaveth no reply, but taketh himself away from that spot, and when next he returneth to the place whereat first the yellow soul spaketh, and whereat upon the day following the day when the soul that is called the ochre one spaketh, and there, also, where the blue spaketh, he made unto himself a cloak of fire as black as inky night, and there did he stretch himself down humbly now upon the earth before Her, and made of himself thereunto a great lamentation and a cry that went up to Her, and this time did his cry availeth, as She did hear him now cry unto Her, and She did marketh and weigh his cry and his lamentation, and She did lifteth him up to Her and bloweth upon him the breath of Her own life . . .' ''*

Professor Prudhomme let out a shriek of laughter that terminated in a high cackle. "And the epistles!" he cried. "There must have been fifty thousand of them on file down in Charles's archives. A brilliant conception. A mail-order goddess! But why not? The woman knew every turn in the road. She had been there! Twenty years in the catacombs! She developed a following! The epistles went out to her postal pilgrims, and you could only guess at the money that came pouring in." The professor flung up his arms. " 'Our Sixth Epistle to Our Novice Marie down in Lunenburg in the Season of her Fleshly Temptations'—'Our Second Epistle to Our Postulant Anne up in Conway on the Occasion of Her Father's Interment.' " Professor Prudhomme clapped a hand to his head in a fit of merriment. "A room of her own?" he cried. "I should think so! She had a church, for the love of Mike! The poor, the sick, the lonelyhearts, the outcasts. Hundreds of them, from Cornwall Bridge to Caribou, Maine.

"Years later, they came to the shrine, to the old jute mill, just to see the place—the cobbled street, the clapboard facade, the faded pink door. And there was Charles Longbottom, in the flesh, dressed up in black-and-gold livery, peeping out at 'em! For two bits, Longbottom took you upstairs to see the shrine—the shabby walls, the little window over the canal, the bed, the dresser, the ink jars, the chamber pot, all of it, and the big *Enosburg Day Book* lying open on the table. He was the keeper, you see. That was his portion. Daphne was gone. Daphne had a twelve-room house up in Richford now, up on the border, the back door of which debouched into Canada, it was said. But before going, she had posted Charles at her cell door, and left him there for all time, a living statue at the open tomb!"

As he didn't know where he was, Professor Prudhomme paused momentarily in his telling, selected a pear from a bowl of fruit shining in the dark before him, and looked about. He had grown accustomed to the pair of slender walnut knees gleaming softly in the dark opposite him. A brass armlet revealed a slender biceps, but the face of the seated figure was cast in shadow. Outdoors, a rain came slashing at the windows.

"And that," said he, "was the Daphne Otis who showed up at Father's farm in 1929, in a little black Cord automobile, brand spanking new, and dressed all elegantly in black—black shoes, black dress, black hat, black veils."

"Quite a picture," said the other.

"Quite a picture, indeed." Professor Prudhomme bit into his pear, and chewed thoughtfully, as his eye floated about the darkness. Bottles winked in a row in an adjoining room, and presently a soft, stoutish figure waddled past the doorway on noiseless feet amid a rustle of satin. Time and again, the rain buffeted the windows, only to withdraw in silvery dancing flashes across a shining asphalt surface.

"Comes the flood," he said.

"Honey, it is," said the other.

"Irony was," the professor continued, chewing with relish now and revolving the bolus of moist pear in his cheek, "that Ida, my own mother, was one of those same lost, woebegone souls grasping at straws that sought a little spiritual solace,

you see, and sat herself down one afternoon to respond by
letter to the magazine clipping that offered a balm and a
blessing for the desperate at heart, a proven way to happiness
among the secret marchers of the Invisible Church. In short,"
the professor bit his lip to stifle a chuckle, "Mama wrote to
her sister. She wrote to Daphne. Ida Prudhomme poured out
her heart to the Invisible Mage, the veiled one, the chief pilgrim
and seer of the Invisible Parish. One could only guess at what
my poor mother committed to paper that autumn day, what
sadnesses and disappointments, but somewhere among the pages
there must have arisen, or been conjured up, the face and
figure of that great honey-haired maiden who came down
from the Memphremagog in the summer of ninety-nine, thirty
years back—that is, a vision of Daphne herself, Daphne the
child, the girl, the beloved sister, the innocent, the open heart,
the true Daphne, the original," Professor Prudhomme said,
"the one who was born to live and to be happy like anyone
else in the world, and was beloved then of Father, and who
bore him a babe, and who was driven out of Eden.

"Talk about your family reunion!" said the professor. "After
we lost Lucinda, Mrs. Prudhomme and I went home for a
spell, first to the Emerson place in Amherst, then on north to
White River. We took the old goat with us, Priscilla's father,
and he rubbing against her all the way, cackling and making
cracks, of course. Hadn't seen her in the summertime in nine
years, and he was so thrilled by it all that his polyps broke out.
We had no sooner got to White River than Mrs. Prudhomme
had to take the old fellow upstairs and treat him with his
powders and his rectal salves. In that same hour, a little black
car stopped at the foot of Father's drive, and just stood there
under the blighted chestnuts, with the sun dancing on its
hood. Ida went outdoors to see. Father was behind her. They
were getting on now, the two of them—Ida, gray-haired, wiping
her hands in her apron, and Father looking a lot like Victor

now, his father, the aquiline nose, the collarless shirt, the big suspenders. But it was Mother who caught a glimpse of the honey hair in the little black automobile, and put her hand to her mouth."

"Daphne," said the other.

"Fate," said the professor.

An outburst of applause followed by several whoops brought Professor Prudhomme through the darkness to the doorway of the room beyond, where a spotlighted black female, tall and spidery, with a scarlet headdress, was just then driving a glass dildo into a yawning pink rump. The lights were amber, then cerise, then lavender, then white, revolving all the while as the dildo was put to work. A wall poster near at hand offered a colorful depiction of SALAMANDRA AND QUEEN ALBERT, the two principals, their names emblazoned in black on a rose ground. When the applause broke out anew, Homer Prudhomme joined in with gusto, clapping and shouting.

As neither performer could drive, Professor Prudhomme took the wheel of the van that night, Salamandra sitting up front beside him, her slim walnut ankles crossed on the dashboard, the air in the cab growing acrid from the yellowish smoke of her cigarette, while Queen Albert lay asleep in the bed in back. The lights of Burlington twinkled through the rain in the depths of the rearview mirror, then winked out with a final breath at a turning in the road. It was then that the woman handed the professor a pear she had shined for him on her crepe skirt. "Get us to Hanover, honey," she said.

"Father," he said, "had just electrified the house. Bought the first radio he ever owned, a big Philco table model, and he and Mother would sit on either side of it, like two cuckoos, bobbing their heads and smiling, without even an inkling of the dark foregathering of spirits taking place that day under the roof of the old farmhouse. Daphne rested herself upstairs in her old room, with the door shut, while Dana Somerset Emerson stretched his bones on the couch in my father's study.

"The drama," Homer Prudhomme went on, "opened about ten o'clock that evening, when we were all six of us sitting about on the screened porch amid Mother's collection of ferns and potted flowers and such, listening to Paul Whiteman's orchestra being broadcast out of the Waldorf-Astoria, Father marveling no end over the genius of our age, when Mother suddenly burst into tears and buried her head in Daphne's lap.

"Daphne," the professor said, "let out a little shriek, an instinctive horror at being *touched,* I suppose, and rid herself of Mother, thrusting Mother from her as though Mother were a lizard that had appeared on her lap. Dana laughed like a maniac as Mother recoiled and ran into the house.

"Daphne was sitting straight up in her chair, her veils trembling but her head perfectly still. You couldn't tell who she was looking at, but Father thought she was looking at him, because he took a wavering step toward the door, then a resolute step toward Daphne. Daphne drew back like that!" Professor Prudhomme straightened himself at the wheel. "Like a cobra!

"That was when you knew that it wasn't love of Ida, or love of Samuel, that had steered Daphne's heart to White River. Priscilla and her father were playing cards on a wicker table, but old Dana had given it up for the moment and was studying Daphne, staring at her with a shiny rocklike eye and a smile on his lips that would terrify a copperhead. Daphne, you see, was gazing back at him. The man was hypnotized. Priscilla saw it, and was worried. She put her hand over Dana's, but he didn't even notice. He was smiling at Daphne.

It made your flesh crawl! Hades looking with lust upon Medusa! You could almost hear their footsteps, the two of them running in league through the labyrinth toward some vile appointment. Somebody was going to be murdered! Somewhere hereabouts a soul was up for grabs! Father was trembling all over, his beard jigging, his trouser legs shaking! Mother of Jesus!" the professor exploded with laughter. "Talk about your lamb being led to the slaughter!

"As for Mrs. Prudhomme, you could bet your bottom dollar she'd never seen the old fornicator look at another woman like that. It scared the daylights out of her. She couldn't concentrate on the cards. They were playing a game that Mrs. Prudhomme had invented for the two of them when she was a girl, during the years following her mother's death, when she was her father's angel, his companion, his comfort—what am I saying?—she was his bed-mate!"

"Watch where you're going." The walnut woman touched the wheel.

"It was called Hearts and Clubs, if memory serves, and was played only with face cards and black deuces." The professor shifted to lower gear for the hill ahead, the wipers beating back and forth against the rain. "I never understood the game, but then neither did anyone else!" He punched the steering wheel gleefully with his fist. "It was the most puzzling game you ever saw—spades and clubs took diamonds, diamonds took hearts, but hearts took spades and clubs. Queens lost to kings but took jacks. Jacks took kings. Deuces were powerless against the king of clubs and queen of hearts, but could capture all ten other picture cards so long as they were led in play rather than being called forth by outcry. Each player was dealt three cards. The remaining cards were stacked facedown in what was called the pit. You drew a card from the pit, then started your own pit by discarding any one of the cards in your hand. That continued till each player had a pit of four cards, yet still held a full hand. Then the pitch began.

"The player that went second in the draw was first to pitch. You followed suit whenever possible. The pitch," Professor Prudhomme explained, "was exciting, particularly as it was accompanied by certain oral ejaculations that were quite original. The old father would fling down a black king, hollering, 'Diamond's daughter!' If Priscilla had the queen of diamonds in hand, she'd have to give it up. If not, however, she might retaliate, as with the king of hearts, or perhaps a jack, thus to collect the king, you see, which went facedown into her pit, and then *she* would lead off the pitch.

"During the pitch, each player knew his opponent's cards, since it was a two-handed game, but couldn't be certain whether a particular card was in hand or in the pit. Priscilla, I noticed, coveted always the queen of hearts, and her father the king of clubs, these two being known as the soul cards, the aim being either to 'deuce' or 'cover' this precious object card, either in one's own pit, or, more dramatically, on the very last play on the board.

"Many was the time," the professor recalled nostalgically, "when this latter eventuality came to pass, with one or the other player, father or daughter, yielding up his soul piece on the last play only to have the other rear back and hurl a king or queen facedown onto the picture card, with a triumphant shout: 'Hearts for clubs!' or 'Clubs to hearts!' or 'King in the pit!' or 'The queen is cooked!' or some such unrestrained cry of triumph.

"Old Dana, like many people who play only one game, was particularly susceptible to shrieking. Mostly, he was very shrewd and calculating throughout the course of the game, his furry eyebrows bunched up like a pair of caterpillars. Some games affected him more than others, and he'd begin to mutter and curse. He'd grind his teeth, and work his feet back and forth on the floor, until about the time of, say, the second or third pitch, when he'd start to groan out loud and bawl at the cards. The veins stood out on his neck, his breathing speeded up, the man's eyes bulged! More than once, the old bedbug worked himself up to such a state that he came to orgasm right there, in the midst of play, dropping his cards and doubling over the table, and howling like a wild animal. That," the professor said, "was the only time you ever saw Mrs. Prudhomme get angry with her dad. Mrs. Prudhomme," Homer added, "could be a stickler for form, you know.

"Father must have known what was coming that night. He didn't even try to go to bed. Mr. Emerson went upstairs, but about midnight he had a nightmare and began smashing furniture up there. Everyone sat on the porch, listening to the violence, as if it had been expected. The old fellow was crying, 'Nichewaug! Nichewaug!' and suddenly he shattered a mirror with a chair. When I got up to his room, he was lying athwart the bed in his longjohns, fast asleep. A vanity mirror was smashed, with the chair actually buried inside it. Mrs. Prudhomme came up behind me. 'Put him to bed, Tup,' she said. 'He'll be shaking and shivering before the night is over.'

"When Ida, my mother, saw that chair driven through the looking glass and right through the frame of the vanity itself, with one leg sticking out the back and another leg broken in two on the floor, she made as if to swoon.

"Father didn't even come upstairs to look! He was standing by his radio on the porch, staring down at Daphne's veils stirring in the night air, and Daphne was speaking to him now, in a soft, hypnotic voice, saying something final and low, like, 'Wrath is just the coming back of the wind, Samuel, chasing itself homeward, blowing its broken horns before it,' and he was nodding, you see, and looking at her. 'Blowing it all along,' she said, 'the leaves and the grains, and the old shoes and tattered baby things.' And Father was nodding, and saying, 'Yes,' and, 'I suppose,' and 'I suppose it would.' And she saying, 'It can be kindly, Samuel, to the hungry and the cheated,' she said 'to the sick and the deformed, letting out the boils and abscesses and the sickness and pus,' and he saying, 'Yes, I suppose, I suppose,' like that. He was in her hands, you see, and knew, too, about the smashing upstairs being just a kind of striking of the great clock at last. And sure enough, after an hour," said the professor, "down came Dana again—about one in the morning now—and he's dressed up in a little black suit and a black derby hat—and out they go together, Dana and Daphne, as nice as you please, to sample the night air.

"You would have thought they all knew something was brewing. Mother was holed up in her room. Father was sitting in his study by the window, looking at his hands. Mrs. Prudhomme had stepped outdoors, and was crying outside the porch screens. Of course, she knew the old swineherd, she knew him backwards and forwards, and knew what it would take to stop him. When they got back to the house, Daphne and Mr. Emerson, Priscilla was sitting out on the porch in her black silk nightgown. The Somersets were silk fetishists, like her cousin, Egan, the blond-haired troglodyte boy from Maine with the big cow-flop feet, who wore brushed silk underpants under his milking britches and silk ankle socks with his boondockers!"

Salamandra touched the wheel. "Watch the road," she said.

"Mrs. Prudhomme was waiting for him, her breasts powdered and perfumed, her face glowing like a seashell in the electric light. After that, they all wanted to be together, and they sat out there, all in black, the three of them, among the ferns and the jardinieres, far into the night, talking and laughing together. Daphne said something about 'lying in after the Second Coming,' and the other two laughed. 'Jesus,' I heard Daphne say, 'wasn't the only one.' '*Jesus?*' the old man cried, just like that, with contempt. 'Jesus was a *boy!*' he cried out, and gave a large frightening laugh, and Daphne," said the professor, "chimed in, *hoo-hooing* like an owl.

"It was about four o'clock in the morning," said he, "when here they come, all three, trooping in single file, and up the stairs, with Daphne leading the way, up to her room. The door shut up there, and you heard the lock being thrown. After that, they were quiet as three mice. What came to pass up there only a witch doctor could guess at, but the next morning Mrs. Prudhomme was walking on her dad's arm, and together they walked with Daphne. They spent the day, the three of them, looking over Father's farm, going about from field to field, in black, with Daphne and Priscilla flanking the little swineherd, each clutching an elbow, and he, with his bowler hat on, very pleased with himself indeed!—and Father," the professor added, "actually following along behind them, about fifty feet back, but as though somehow connected to them, like the tail of a three-headed creature, stopping when they stopped, going when they did, and stopping and going, and so on. Completely out of his mind! Just a ghost, you see.

"They didn't look back. They didn't need to. They knew he was there. They glided in through the woodlots, and then out across the open meadows, and on under the row of the dead chestnut trees, with Father following like a shadow, stopping and going, stopping and going, and on into the woodlots again.

"He was finished, you see. They were pulling him along, as if through the landscape of the years, through a lifetime of toil, of going back and forth on the selfsame pathways and furrows and rows of spring upon spring and fall upon fall, and on in, like that, they came, the three of them, moving almost in step, floating in across the yard and then straight in at the big gaping doorway of the barn, with Daphne's and Priscilla's black dresses blowing in the October wind, and Daphne's veils rising and settling, and right on into the darkness of Father's barn, and dissolving in there, the three of them, in the gloom. Father paused in the doorway, standing there in his collarless white shirt and big Sunday suspenders, and his beard pointing the way in, but his feet stopped in the mud. He just stood there. After a moment, a half-dozen little piglets came racing out of the barn, squirting every which way under his feet, going like the devil this way and that.

"Of course, Father had to go in. It was in the cards, you might say, in the hearts and the clubs. But he was of more than one mind about it. This was the sacred doorway, after all. And he remembered—how could he not?—sitting here in the blue twilights, dreaming on Wenonah," said the professor, "tall as the prairie lily, daughter of Nokomis. And of Daphne, their coming out together on horseback, her hair blowing a golden net about his face, their two fowling pieces pointing to the heavens. It was all up now. For Father, the happy times were over and gone, I'm afraid.

"Samuel Prudhomme! The last American plowman, the last tiller, yeoman, mower, woodcutter, drover, and jack-of-all-trades. Just a solitary figure in worn trousers and a white shirt, standing in the doorway of the stalls, rick, and granary of an entire age! Squinting in at it!

"He went in, following them. Knew where they were, I suppose. It was his appointment, not mine. At supper, he couldn't cut his meat! Mother helped him with his cup. The man couldn't unbutton his shirt. God knows what he saw.

"I looked in on him in the middle of the night. I opened his door. Father was on his hands and knees in the moonlight, and she was standing over him. She was wearing Priscilla's black silk nightgown. Or," said the professor, "it was Priscilla holding up Daphne's mask. I never knew. Either way, the man was finished. You'd have thought a freight train was coming at him. Mind you," said the professor, "his time was up. No two ways about it. All the rest was just metaphor, you might say, a certain specificity, the poetry of the hard facts, one form the same as the next.

"Daphne come back from the dead! That's not bad!"

Professor Prudhomme crowed. "A fertility goddess wanting a face. That's not bad! It could have been otherwise. But does it matter? If you're going to be run over by a locomotive, does it matter if you've got your pants on straight! He was five payments in arrears at the bank.

"When Daphne Otis came floating down the front stairs that night, looking for her Pepto-Bismol, and somebody," the professor said, "was still upstairs in her room, *hoo-hooing* like an owl, does it matter that it wasn't Aunt Daphne?

"Mrs. Prudhomme knew theater! She could play the part! It wasn't that. It just didn't matter. You see, all that matters," the professor said, "was that Daphne Otis bought up Father's mortgage. His labors were hers, and Mother's rotted gazebo was hers, and the house and the barns and every whippoorwill that nested on the place. And even *that*," Homer cried, "didn't matter. Because in a month's time, the markets were breaking worldwide, from Sherbrooke to Shanghai.

"It was over. There was no demand for his produce, his milk, his poultry. His tools were obsolete. His habits were obsolete. His way of talking was obsolete! His clothing, his diet, his beliefs. Life lost meaning," the professor said. "The look in the eye of a cow. The timing of lilacs. The different kinds of rain.

"The only thing Father got to keep was Zillah, a big black mare that stood seventeen hands at the withers. Mother went off her chump," the professor concluded, "and Father was left alone with Zillah. However you slice it, it was the beginning of a time of want.

"Still," he said airily, "the visit ended on an agreeable note. That often happens, you know. There was laughter and merriment. For one thing, old Dana got dressed up to the nines one morning, and took Priscilla riding with him in his Buick up to Vershire. Said he wanted to marry her! Probably did, too! The old fox!

"Mother, who still didn't know that Daphne was more like a deity now than anything else, and ran a strict bedehouse up in Richford for a bunch of mum's-the-word anchorites who prayed to her in chapel every night and put up jellies for sale to the A&P in the daytime—Mother made a confession of her own. She said that twenty-nine years ago she had made a changeling of her baby. For about ten minutes," said the professor, "I thought I was Lemuel Otis. Not that it hadn't occurred to me before. But Daphne set Mother to rights on that point, explaining how she knew all about that, and had changed the babes back again. Daphne then gave Mother to realize that, so far as she, Daphne, was concerned, Ida and Samuel Prudhomme were just a couple of rustics who happened to be in the vicinity when she, Daphne, had given birth to the 'god who was not meant to be.'

"Everyone laughed heartily," said Professor Prudhomme, "when Aunt Daphne, sitting in her Cord automobile, preparing to go, looked up at me through her mask. 'If I were his mother,' she said, 'would I tell the world?'"

The walnut woman's scarlet headdress shimmered in the winter sun as she led the way in barbaric splendor down the middle of Main Street between the man-tall snowdrifts. Her dark skin glowed like fire among the leather interstices of her harnesslike costume. Immediately at her heels came her plump, satin-footed servant, carrying her fur coat and embroidered faldstool. Professor Prudhomme brought up the rear. They marched single file into the Latchis Hotel to breakfast, where Queen Albert made a ceremonious show of fawning over the spidery Negress as she seated herself.

"I slept seven winters in the barn," said Professor Prudhomme, "so that Mrs. Prudhomme could show her old dad the meaning of daughterly love. May God strike me dead," he insisted, "from the Eve of All Souls to Groundhog Day, from his birthday to hers, and never clapped eyes on them but once, that unfortunate Christmas night, in the snowfall, in the window, when she lay, statuesque, in silks upon the table, and he was showing young Egan, who died in the nightclub fire, how to fondle and arouse a woman."

"Why don't you take off your coat!" Queen Albert said, and then appealed to Salamandra. "Tell him to take off his coat! We'll be thrown out of here."

"I stuck to my last," said the professor. "I read every book, poem, monograph, and magazine ever printed. I earned two degrees up in the barn! 'You can gobble,' Mrs. Prudhomme said, 'you can teach crowing!' Why not, said I!"

"It's a disgrace," said Queen Albert, mortified by the old man's coat.

"In 1935, Mrs. Prudhomme did a Miss Olive Chancellor for a young Cabot boy at the Ritz-Carlton that you couldn't get today for a million dollars. You'd've sworn," Homer Prudhomme said, "she was his mom! Or even his grandmom! With her silver-rimmed specs and her walking shoes. Until she reached under the table and got hold of him! Christ Jesus, did that boy sit up!"

Salamandra touched Professor Prudhomme's arm. "Eat your grapefruit."

"Cost him an arm and leg, too! Of course, Mrs. Prudhomme made small of it. 'Nouns have to verb, *even,*' she said, 'a wee cockalorum of a Cabot!' " The professor went off into a fit of wheezing and coughing while thumping his spoon on the table.

Queen Albert showed Salamandra a pinched look. "May I eat *also?*"

"Then the war came," said the professor, "and Robert sown along with it, back in thirty-seven, around Halloween, and the old cockroach dead in February."

"Seems to me," Queen Albert snapped, "that's about the third time in three years that that cockroach died."

"One death is not enough for some," said the majestic Negress, seated on her own special chair.

"The rest is history." Professor Prudhomme pushed back his moth-eaten coat sleeves and attacked his grapefruit. "Down in the cockpit, tearing themselves to pieces," he said, "the redshirts and the blackshirts, the blackshirts and the brown-shirts, the Kings and the Popes, the Reds and the Whites, Latins and Slavs, Christians and Jews, the priests and Gaulei-ters and commissars! Do you know, Mrs. Prudhomme couldn't look at a mushroom cloud without thinking about old Dana and his polyps!" The professor threw down his spoon in sudden gaiety. "Marjorie got a headstone up in Pelham, but they *buried* her," he said, "under the dahlia bed by the summer-kitchen door! You could dig it up. That's history!" he said. "That's life!

"I haven't been following the frost line up and down the piedmont for ten thousand years for nothing!" Professor Prudhomme looked up in confusion. "I want my wife!" he cried.

On the seventh of June, Professor Prudhomme crossed the border into Massachusetts at Hoosac Tunnel, descended to Zoar, and started up through the high woods of East Hawley for home. By nightfall, he was going lickety-split through the wooded outskirts of Amherst, off course by a degree, but talking and laughing animatedly, when he crossed paths with Mr. Thad Mungo, a long-headed hermit of the neighborhood. Mr. Mungo, coming rapidly forward on birdlike legs, emerged suddenly to view around the bole of an oak tree, and smashed into the white-haired poet with a force that sent him sprawling. Mercifully, Homer Prudhomme lit on a moss-bed.

"Nothing offends like a foul smell," said the professor, "and nothing is so fetid as the stink of a man!"

Mr. Mungo, wavering on skinny, black-trousered legs set wide apart, directed his words no less pointedly at the man sprawled before him in the dark. "The housekeeper," said Mr. Mungo, "liked to tell about the yellow-haired British tar who came to call in the summer of 1917. A beautiful boy come straight from a man-o'-war docked in Boston harbor."

"So long as the father was not in the house," said the professor, "it was no great matter, since the daughter was running in and out with cut flowers perpetually. With roses, with lilacs, with peonies, and such! Their perfumes fought the battle all day long to kill the stench left over from the night before!"

"Boy's name was Reginald Royce," Mr. Mungo recalled, as he laid his bony hand pensively to his face and appeared to be considering the stars peeping forth over the treetops. "Reginald Royce. I haven't heard that name spoken in a dog's age. And what a boy! What a lovely boy! A boy of the Empire! A good solid lad, with an easy smile, and yes, as smart-looking in his dress whites as Admiral Jellicoe himself. Reginald Royce was the walking promise of life!"

"There are odors," said Professor Prudhomme, "that excite a repugnance in every cell of the human body. The reek of a corpse, for one, the singular odor of excrement—rotted smells that incite aversion, recoil, flight! When Dana Somerset Emerson made his way to the dinner table, pulling himself up to sit, flipping back the tails of his cutaway, the reek came up from his clothes like a disembowelment!"

"If you had known the girl in the summer of that year," Mr. Mungo leveled a finger at him, "if you had seen her walking on the highway, or scouring the woodlots for vervain, apple-peru, jack-in-the-pulpit, why, you would have believed that virginity had found a vessel in which it might repose forever. There were lavender lights in her cheekbones! Her hair was raven! She was magical. Her name was spoken in whispers. People used to say it was the spirit of Emily Dick herself come back to Amherst and the world, but endowed this time around with physical attributes appropriate to her uplifted nature."

"Outdoors, the frogs were whomping away in their thousands," said the professor. "I tell you, it was hot! My head was spinning. The room was filled with the drone of houseflies, drawn, you understand, to the smell of their natural breeding grounds. The girl was sitting at the foot of the table, with her white neck gleaming behind a cluster of blue iris."

"You would not want to look into her eyes," said Mr. Mungo, raising his voice. "You would not want to be touched by her fingers. You would not dare! Everyone knew the story of the weasel-faced man who lived with the pigs on the hill—a cousin of the daughter, who had come to call! and whom the father, in his wickedness, had bade stay!" Thad Mungo raised high his incredibly long arms to signify the heights of human evil. "And yet," he exclaimed, "was I not myself bewitched? And what of the housekeeper, the woman who was forbidden ever to employ her broken English even though her native Cornish tongue was, in that year, 1917, *extinct* across the face of the globe, save for the one solitary exception in all the world, her own unique, isolated, infinitely forlorn grumblings and prayers!" Mr. Mungo produced a hoot of laughter, his ashy head glowing momentarily in the moonlight. "I'd call that bewitched! The old woman was gone beyond recall. Terror and beauty a wondrous prison make. Yes, *I* was enchanted," said Mr. Mungo, "but I hadn't the timber to beard the lion in his den, nor anything approaching it. I was not Reginald Royce! I was not so pure. I was not so heroic. I was not so beautiful, nor," he said, with irony, "was I so god-awful dumb!"

"It was like dining with a pestilence, with a corpse, with the Devil himself." Professor Prudhomme nodded perfunctorily, as if acknowledging Mr. Mungo's agreement with his own words. "Between the chorus of frogs outside the dining-room windows and the befouled air scalding my eyes, I might have wondered where on earth I was! And yet," the professor turned up a palm, foretokening a contrary line of reasoning, "the daughter was always praising of the man, always solicitous, always looking across the table to him for the rejoinder that he never made, for the smile that he never gave. She told him who I was," said the professor, "and where I came from, and where I was going. They sat at either end of the table in two massive carven chairs, while I, the stranger, was given a little Chippendale seat from the parlor that placed me at a visible disadvantage. I was wearing my old army uniform but with white shoes and a sky-blue necktie! White shoes! The marvel of it. Of course, I was tongue-tied! If anything saved me, I suppose it was my face. It was a boy's face," said Professor Prudhomme, "but it was battered."

"I saw that young Britisher with my own two eyes," Mr. Mungo allowed. "I saw him arrive. I did not," he specified gravely, "see him leave."

"I had barbed-wire scars from here to here! I had broken teeth! When I came home from France, my mother looked at me and wept. My father turned away!"

Mr. Mungo extended a long arm toward the town, the lights of which shone faintly through the trees. "I saw him come up the hill from the train station and stride out across the Amherst green. His hair was corn-ripened yellow, his bearing a thing of beauty. Women," said Mr. Mungo, "stopped in the street. Workmen set down their tools. The boy was Christly. I tell you, the sun didn't shine but it shone on Reginald Royce. He was a vision in white. The man simply walked off a canvas. You might have supposed—indeed, I often have supposed—that he was the product of a powerful wish. That she had cast a wish, like an invisible fishline, far out onto God's blue ocean, and that he, young Mr. Royce, was just made into flesh out there! On the deeps!"

"I needn't have felt shy," said Professor Prudhomme. "In those past weeks, since that Friday in June, she and I had made love more times and in more different ways than a millipede could count on his shinbones! Now I had proposed marriage to her!"

"There was a war going on. *You* remember," Thad Mungo charged. "You're no spring chicken! Young ladies everywhere were knitting socks and mittens and sending out letters and packages to boys in every branch of the service from here to God knows where, and who," he asked, "should fall recipient to one of Miss Emerson's own magical gifts?" Mr. Mungo brought down his head. "A British gunner named Reginald Royce!"

"Let me go back a few hours to the afternoon," said the professor, "when we walked in silence together through the rooms of her father's house. I didn't touch her. We didn't so much as brush bodies. She showed me her chinaware, her silver, her linens. She smiled over the silliness of her possessions. She showed me her ferns. We walked together, side by side, passing from room to room, moving in that silent conjunction that is the perfection," he said, "of planets. In an upstairs room, we paused at the foot of a bed, and there," he said, "she told me what no mortal had ever heard from her lips. She would marry her soul to mine for all time to come, she said, for time and eternity. 'Honor me,' she said. 'It is my soul that will love you, Tup, for time and eternity.' She spoke these words to me. We stood at the foot of the bed in which she was born, the bed where the old scorpion nightly defiled her—an arrangement not then known to me, I hasten to say. The bed," Professor Prudhomme recalled, "was itself stupendous, a great wonderwork in black hickory. I looked upon it, I swear, with the wonder of a Jason, or a Perseus, of one who had withstood the trials, who had survived the wire entrapments and the poisonous fumes, the mangling and the killing, to attain at last the high dark meadows, to enter at last into the dwelling place of the old fornicator's noble daughter!"

Thad Mungo smiled with satisfaction. "Yes, it's my own idea," he said, "that he came blowing over the sea to her door as the ancient sailors followed the sweet, fatal lure of the Sirens, calling them to their ruin. It was her seventeenth summer, and I," he attested, "and every right-thinking Yankee lad from here to Windsor Jams was head over heels in love with the girl. The nights I tossed and turned!" Mr. Mungo marched about in a tight circle, limp with amusement. "The dreams in which she came to me. The bedclothes that I soiled!

The nights I walked these roads. Oh, many was the summer night," he proclaimed, "when I slept right here beneath this red oak tree."

"Outdoors," the professor said, "she took my arm, and questioned me politely about my family and ancestry. I told her that my father, Samuel, was a rural philosopher, a man for whom farming was an act of reverence, a man who, like Daniel Webster himself, loved his horses so much that he buried them standing up in full harness! I asked had she ever been proposed marriage to. She said yes, by men who did not come up to the mark. She asked then had I ever proposed marriage to another. I replied that I had not. She smiled at me from the corner of her eye. In a sudden access of feeling," Professor Prudhomme grew excited, "I told her that I had never known any other woman in the carnal way, not even one, and what was even more noteworthy, particularly up around White River Junction in those days, that I had never been intimate with any mammal whatsoever!" The professor loosed a happy shout.

"I," Mr. Mungo confessed, "followed her once. I saw her on the cart road above the lumber camp, moving dreamlike in the shadows of the cedars. Marjorie, the hag, followed behind at a respectful distance. The old Cornish cook was carrying a wicker-basket with greens inside it. Miss Emerson carried a pair of steel snips. My heart was beating like a drum."

"She was twenty years old," said the professor. "She was wearing something blue with white spots, and a narrow white sash that she wove through her fingers as we talked. We came up to the slaughterhouse door," said the professor, "and she said me the words again! 'It is my soul that will love you for time and eternity!' She left me there and walked back to the house. The door closed behind her." Professor Prudhomme sat pouting, with his legs spread before him.

"I followed her no farther," said Mr. Mungo, "and you

wouldn't have, either, my friend. The destroyed look on the face of the old crone toiling along in the leaves behind her would have given the boldest man pause. No, I wasn't Reginald Royce," he said. "The afternoon Royce appeared, the old woman was down on her knees with a pail and brush, scrubbing the stones, and she just froze there, on all fours, looking up. Standing down in the roadway was a youth, dressed all in white, straight and still as a fence post, staring up at the house. He had come, you see! And wasn't it a day for heroes! A summer day," said Mr. Mungo, "so hot and sultry that a breeze in the meadows would lift up butterflies by the basketful. She could have been a graven brute crouched on all fours at the temple door. Young Miss Emerson came outdoors behind her, shading her eyes from the sun, and holding an armful of roses and lupine. She took Mr. Royce indoors. She held his arm. She walked him about the rooms. Young as she was, she was stately, decorous, beautifully composed."

"I found her without looking," said Homer Prudhomme, "but I can't tell you how I did it. I went straight to her. I went in at the door of the summer kitchen, stepped over the legs of the old scrubwoman, and went up the back stairs. I knew where she was, and I knew she was waiting for me. I had an instinct for her, a sixth sense, something running in the blood. I always have had. I knew where she was. We had gone through the house together like children at a game, at hopscotch, hopping from block to block. I knew where she was because, you see, we hadn't been there. We had missed a block! Something conspicuous by its absence. By then, I was actually running," he said, "straight up the attic steps to the door. She wanted me to do that. I could feel it! I could feel her heart beating in my own chest! I opened the door," Professor Prudhomme said, "and I saw her!"

"I've never been inside the house," said Mr. Mungo, "but it was a big, stuffy, old-fashioned house, with dark wall colors, heavy rugs, tall mahogany furnishings. Where the daylight managed to leak in, it was collected at once by something metallic, a little glimmering," he said, "a brass clock, a pewter vase, a fire-dog, something proclaiming its existence by reflection. The two of them walked side by side through the rooms, not touching, but moving together like parts of a single function. The air, often tinged with certain heavy scents that we associate with farm life, was perfumed today by a hundred cut blossoms. No," sang Mr. Mungo, as he began to pace in the moonlight, "Reginald Royce was not a fellow from hereabouts, someone to be—well—cracked on the head with a shovel, let's say. He was a suitor in the old high way. He held His Majesty's commission! They sat together," he said, "Reginald and she, in two fine chairs by the parlor fireplace, one to the left and one to the right, the glory of the Empire, the flower of the Republic."

"If the Grail had eyes," said Professor Prudhomme, "and longed to be recovered, here was its living form. She was sitting in a pine rocker at the foot of a child's bed. Her patent shoes lay tumbled to one side. It was her original bedchamber. It was in this low-ceilinged dusty room seven years back that she'd heard the beating of the wings of the great cockfather. Here he flew down. You can't know what I'm talking about. But I knew. Knew something. That was in the afternoon. In the evening we sat in darkness at the table. The father spoke strangely. He watched me. He talked on subjects that made my flesh crawl. He talked about the intelligence of rats. Rats! I went him one better! The girl was watching us, her eyes going back and forth behind the flowers. I told him about the rats of France, how they propagated in the trenches after every attack!" The professor shouted at Mr. Mungo. "I told about the human eye in the belly of the rat I chopped in two with a shovel!"

"I am trying to talk!" Mr. Mungo shouted.

"After that, he didn't want to talk about rats. No," said the professor, "he wanted to talk about snakes, about adders and rattlers and copperheads, and what a blue racer would do to a rattlesnake every time! He said he had a feeling for snakes. An affinity."

Mr. Mungo formed a tent of his fingers and placed his hands across his nose, peering over his fingertips at the seated figure before him. "That afternoon," he continued, "Reginald Royce asked for the young lady's hand in marriage. They were standing on the paving stones at the back of the house. The housekeeper, laboring on her hands and knees in the summer kitchen, pricked up her ears. They were standing just beyond the screens, she in blue, the sailor in white."

"I gave him snakes," Homer Prudhomme snickered and caught at his breath. "I told him about the snake sandwiches that Junior and Henry Ballou made for their grandpa! The old coot sitting up in the open loft door of the barn, not a tooth in his head, munching it down, licking his fingers. The old donkey thought it was sardines!"

"Miss Emerson didn't reply," Mr. Mungo continued softly. "She kept him waiting. Instead, she asked the young Britisher about his family and his antecedents. She smiled at him from the corner of her eye. She took him indoors and showed him in an upstairs room the bed she was born in. She showed him the big hickory siege perilous by the stairhead and her collection of ferns. He was smitten! He had fallen in love with the girl as a man falls in love with the ocean, or with an entire people!"

"That night," Homer Prudhomme recalled, "I was put up in the front upstairs bedroom, a room once occupied by a family ancestor named Remember Garland. Remember, they said, knew more about hogs than all the hog raisers in China. They said he could breed hogs in such a way they would give birth to porcupines if he wanted them to. His only failure, they said, was when he tried to cross a pig with a turkey. Instead of getting pigs with wings, which was what he wanted, he got little turkey chicks armed with tusks!" The professor laughed over his own humor. "I was just sitting up in bed, smoking my cob pipe, and studying the oil portrait of Remember hanging over the mantel, when I heard, I thought, the girl's voice. My mind was full of her, filled up with thoughts of the doings of that summer day, and I got up and went to the door."

"At dinner," said Mr. Mungo, "the father and daughter sat at either end of the table in great hickory chairs, like a king and queen, while Royce of His Majesty's Royal Navy pulled up on a chair of no special pedigree. There were daffodils. There was candlelight. Miss Emerson's legendary face shone through the candlelit flowers, itself a flower," said Mr. Mungo, "a white orchid on a white stalk. As always, the room was touched by odors redolent of the barnyard. Her old father sat up lightly in his chair, as certain growths, I believe, affected his sitting."

"I saw him," the professor said. "The door to her room stood ajar, and I saw him making his way past the stairhead, coming from the lavatory. He was wearing longjohns from the waist down. His chest and arms were naked. The hair on his head stood up in a shock! His two feet stuck out of his underwear like soap-colored hooves. But that was nothing. All of that was naught, a mere canvas upon which was painted the picture of a Yankee satyr, when compared to the rest of it! An instrument so enormous," he shouted, "that you would have thought you had not seen aright!" The professor threw forward his entire forearm and fist. "It was standing outside of his underwear, like that! The cock came out of him like a living tree! An eruption so big, so unmanlike, that the mere sight of it would have sent a mare crashing in terror through the stable walls!" The professor swung his fists about. "I heard them! I heard the sound of it! Of the two bodies! The moon came through the door like a white fire. The room was white on fire! I stumbled. I dropped backward into a chair at the stairhead. I could see them! I was bolted to the chair, and I was still alive, still breathing! Her arms wound around him. Her legs wound around him. I couldn't move. I was speech-less. I was staring into the furnace, don't you understand!"

"He was terrified of snakes!" Mr. Mungo's voice rose dramatically. "They all three detected it, even the house-keeper, who was clearing the table. The word *snakes* sent an icicle up his British backbone! The old woman said that as long as she lived, she would never again wish to see painted on the face of mortal man the look she saw upon the father later that night when he came indoors." Mr. Mungo reached out his left hand and dangled down his fingers. "From between these fingers," he said, "hung three living snakes clasped by the tail. The father came in at the back door of the house sometime after midnight, with three striped adders squirming down from his fingers, and with that brutal look upon his face, and up the stairs he went. The yellow-haired boy lay sleeping in a room at the front of the house."

"I was afflicted with buzzing sounds, dizzy spells, seeing double!" said the professor.

"Reginald Royce, you see," said Mr. Mungo, "had run upon the rocks of his own special fate. What happened, precisely, I cannot say, but it may be assumed that the old villain made him a companion of vipers in his bed. Up with the counter-pane, and a flick of the wrist. That would have done it." Mr. Mungo winked. "It would have done it for many a man. No one saw the boy depart," said Mr. Mungo, as he turned to go, "but depart he surely did."

"She kissed me on the lips," said Professor Prudhomme, "and in a way she saved me, freed me, just, I suppose, as she was saved in me. Those ebony eyes wrote the very signature on Christ's prayer for human mercy. She wanted nothing more than a cup of mercy. Not God's mercy. Nothing so grand. Maybe there is mercy enough in the mercy of a boy in white shoes from White River Junction. I don't know. I was clutching the arms of the chair. She came to me. She kissed me on the lips. I understood," he said. "I accepted her."

Just before midnight, the station-house door opened, and the couple returned from the street, the big white-haired lady carrying the luggage for the two of them, her companion on her arm. "Trouble with honeymoons," she was saying, in a mellow baritone, "you've got to stretch them out and bang them without letting 'em know that that's what it's all about. You," she told him, "got to get used to making Mother happy."

"*I* like affection, too," the man said, as he wiped frost from the window glass and peered up the darkened tracks through the falling snow.

"Affection is what you show your dog," said the woman.

"Love, then!" the man exclaimed, peevishly.

"At three o'clock in the morning," she said, "I don't want my little sunflower up reading and smoking cigarettes."

"Oh, *that,*" the other tossed out. "Is that what's put you in such a state?"

Professor Prudhomme was trying to hear. He didn't know where on earth he was. He was confused by the snow.

"Am I imagining it," said the golden-haired fellow, "or is that a person?"

At that, he and the big woman turned their eyes to the row of oaken benches.

"That's the stove," she said.

The Flower of the Republic

. . .

Outdoors, the night was balmy. No one was about. He was standing, not on a platform, but on solid ground, at the place where the road and the returning trees blended. There was water in the distance. Beyond that, a light in the forest.

The girl standing in the doorway was simpleminded.

"This is Nichewaug," she said. "Nichewaug is a wilderness. I have a map, but we're not on it. You were sleeping," she said. "So was I. I live with Mrs. Hummison."

The professor's hair was disheveled from sleep. The room was white and the bed was white, as were the curtains, bedcovers, his pajamas. Everything was white. A white lamp depended on a white chain from the ceiling.

"Mrs. Hummison says if I could read I could go to school, but I can't. I can print, and I can draw, and I can talk," the girl said. "I can cook and I can count money. I pay Mr. Miles for Mrs. Hummison. She calls Mr. Miles on the telephone, and he comes in the afternoon at four o'clock in a green car."

She came then a tentative step into the room. She had long black hair and crooked teeth. "I'm Sybil," she said. "Mrs. Hummison would like to know who you are. She can't get up. I told her what you looked like. Especially your hair. You have pretty hair," she said.

Professor Prudhomme awoke in the afternoon to the pressure of a warm hand under his back, drawing him forward. He was drinking milk. The girl was holding the glass to his lips. He knew she had done this before. He remembered the warmth of her hand, an imprint there, and more than once. Many times.

"Mrs. Hummison was born here. This is the only house in Nichewaug. That's why Mr. Miles brings the mail. Do you know what day it is?" The girl leaned and wiped his lips with the blanket. "Wednesday. And yesterday was Tuesday." She paused. She was standing near to him. "Mrs. Hummison keeps a calendar. She receives money once a month. You drank it all," the girl said. "I'll tell Mrs. Hummison."

She was back momentarily. "You can look out your window," she said. "A long time ago, Mr. Hummison had a barn. I've been here three years. There was an orchard, too. I never saw it. Those," she said, looking out, "are poplars. If you sit up, you can see the fern-beds."

The girl stood in the middle of the room with her hands clasped at her waist, her elbows to her body, her feet together precisely. The sun dimmed at the window, and grew bright. The curtains moved, then settled back. Professor Prudhomme closed and opened his eyes.

"Mrs. Hummison heard you at the window. I brought you indoors. There are three of us in this house now. You spoke in your sleep," she said. "I listened. You said, 'When Father was a babe-in-arms, he found himself one afternoon in a rowboat.'"

Professor Prudhomme made an effort to stir, but failed.

"I take care of you," the girl said. "When I go to read the gas, you will see me outside the window." She smiled, going out, and, after a minute, reappeared in the sun outdoors. She went past the window, then came back again. Her hair shone like coal in the sun. A door slammed.

Sybil played with dolls. She bathed and dressed them, and taught them how to talk. She was up at dawn. He heard her moving about. She came and lifted his legs, and gave him a pan. The house was silent, except for the rattle and hiss of his water. She went away, and came back, and went away. Then she was standing in the doorway, just as yesterday, with the sun on her shoes. Professor Prudhomme lay on his back, cherry-faced against the white, his runny eyes fixed upon her.

"I gave you Mr. Hummison's pajamas," she said. "He wore white pajamas in summer, and blue ones in the winter. His slippers are in a box. Mr. Hummison was a schoolteacher. Mrs. Hummison has a picture of him. I can tell stories," the girl said. "I'm thirteen."

Again, as she had the day before, the girl advanced a step into the room, and stood there, with her hands clasped at her waist, her feet together, her head high. "Mrs. Hummison," she said, "would like to know who you are. No one comes to Nichewaug. When Mrs. Hummison dies, I will go away. I'm the only child in Nichewaug. Mrs. Hummison's son was killed in the war, in the east. I was born in the east. I was born in Wheelwright."

The girl was watching him intently. She was standing now in the center of the room, the sun on her shoes. She wetted her lips, and her eyes widened and grew dark. He sensed the power of what was to come. He could all but feel it. The girl was eyeing him gravely. A light entered her eyes. Her lips twisted, revealing a slanted tooth.

"Junior had snowshoes," she said, "made out of alder saplings and rawhide."

Professor Prudhomme squeezed the bedsheet between his fingers. The girl moistened her lips.

"Junior and I had a lean-to up at Brandon Gap. One winter night, Henry came up to camp to say that Father was home from Hanover and had brought a black colt with him. A beautiful animal," she said.

The girl stood in the center of the room, her gaze and the

gaze of the old man reaching through the dark that came down.

He was talking, then, in the darkness, touching her hand. She sat in a rocker, a silhouette against the window glass, listening.

"I looked back," he said. "Like Orpheus. I began to speak. I couldn't stop. I remembered. She was lying in the dark upon the table, in silks, I said, her hair spread in a fan about her head, her hands like two orchids above her belly, like sculpture, like glass."

"I looked back," said the girl. "Like Orpheus. I began to speak—"

"Like the wife of Lot."

"Like the wife of Lot. I began to speak. I couldn't stop. I remembered. She was lying in the dark upon the table, in silks, I said, her hair spread in a fan about her head, her hands like two orchids above her belly, like sculpture."

"Like glass."

"Like glass," she said.

"I lost her."

"I spoke," she said.

"I spoke."

Raymond Kennedy, the son of a printer, was reared in New England and was educated at the University of Massachusetts. He has written for the stage and has brought out three previous novels, *My Father's Orchard, Good Night, Jupiter,* and *Columbine.* He is also the author of "Room Temperature," a short story that has won exceptional praise. He currently makes his home in Brooklyn with his wife and young daughter.

A NOTE ON THE TYPE

This book was set in a film version of Granjon, a type named in compliment to Robert Granjon, but neither a copy of a classic face nor an entirely original creation. George W. Jones based his designs for this type on that used by Claude Garamond (1510–61) in his beautiful French books, and Granjon more closely resembles Garamond's own type than do any of the various modern types that bear his name.

Composed by Centennial Graphics, Inc.,
Ephrata, Pennsylvania
Printed and bound by R. R. Donnelly & Sons, Co.,
Harrisonburg, Virginia

Typography and binding design by
Dorothy Schmiderer